"You were ███████████
Mattie. Yo█████████████

Eyes narrowed, she pulled away from him. Despite the scare, Dom had no say in how she chose to describe the incident or what she did about it. "I *am* fine."

She had a fairly even temperament, she truly did, but Dominic was making her emotions bounce from one extreme to the other. He'd made it quite clear what he thought of her ten years ago. Granted, she'd probably speeded his rejection along, but she'd been scared. She'd wanted him safe, even if that meant giving up his dream job. After all, she'd thought she was his dream, too.

Obviously not, since he'd certainly dropped her quick enough when things had started to get complicated.

"You're not afraid of me anymore," Dom said quietly.

"I was never afraid of you." Afraid of the feelings he inspired, sure, but not of him.

The barely-there smile suddenly radiated pure arrogance. "Prove it. Have dinner with me."

* * *

Dear Reader,

The year 2011 has been a dream come true in many ways, including the release of my debut novel with Harlequin Romantic Suspense. I feel beyond privileged to be working with a publishing house where so many great authors first started their careers. I can still remember reading Linda Howard's *Diamond Bay* (back when the Harlequin Romantic Suspense line was still Intimate Moments) and immediately launching a mission to find the previous book, *Midnight Rainbow.* Those two books are still on my "keeper shelves," and I aspire to be an author on one of your keeper shelves someday, too!

Dom and Mattie's story is particularly special to me because I was able to use my experiences as a criminal prosecutor to add authenticity to the courtroom settings. Plus, I've always been fascinated by the idea of young lovers who connect a little too early and are torn apart, but then, after growing and living and learning what really matters to them, are able to reunite so that their bond is not just stronger, but unbreakable.

Every book I write is meant to inspire and empower the belief that our capacity for love and goodness never dies. I'd love to hear from you! You can always reach me at virna@virnadepaul.com.

Wishing you much love, happiness and reading pleasure,

Virna DePaul

VIRNA DEPAUL

Dangerous to Her

ROMANTIC
SUSPENSE

Recycling programs
for this product may
not exist in your area.

ISBN-13: 978-0-373-27744-5

DANGEROUS TO HER

www.Harlequin.com

Printed in U.S.A.

Books by Virna DePaul

Harlequin Romantic Suspense
Dangerous to Her #1674

VIRNA DEPAUL

was an English major in college and, despite a passion for Shakespeare, Broadway musicals and romance novels, somehow ended up with a law degree. For ten years, she was a criminal prosecutor for the state of California. Now she's thrilled to be writing stories about complex individuals (fully human or not) who are willing to overcome incredible odds for love.

Although I conceived this story, I owe its birth to the family and friends who've always supported me, and to those who, in recent years, have become part of my writing family. In particular, thank you to my agent and editor, Holly Root and Mary-Theresa Hussey, my critique partners, and my boys, Joshua, Ethan, and Zachary. Finally, I dedicate this book to Craig, my first, best and only, always and forever, for helping me sprout wings.

Chapter 1

"Joel's dead."

Dominic Jeffries stared at fellow detective Cameron Blake, wondering if he was dreaming. It was only a little after six in the morning, less than eight hours since he'd finished his latest undercover op, and he had stopped by to have a quick drink with his best friend, Joel Bustamante. Despite Dom having been gone for six months, their drink together had been quick because Dom had been focused on getting three things: a bed to sleep in, a woman to hold for a few hours, and then his next assignment before he was tempted to examine his life and exactly where it was going a little too closely. Likewise, Joel, a newly promoted sergeant and perpetually starry-eyed honeymooner, had been anxious to get back home to his new wife, Tawny.

After talking business and then listening to Joel extol the virtues of settling down with one woman, Dom had finally gotten the bed, had lost interest in the woman, and had been prepared to nail down his next assignment—and not the one Joel had wanted him to take—later today.

Now? Standing in his living room, shirtless and in baggy sweats, his hair falling in eyes that were still half-blurry, Dom locked his knees to keep them from collapsing.

He'd had a brief premonition of trouble before leaving Joel last night. Hard not to given Joel's ultimatum that Dom finally take some time off or settle for babysitting a judge who might be dirty, in danger or neither. Still, Dom had dismissed the premonition as paranoia. After all, he'd just spent six months living in deep cover with a group of ruthless criminals. But not once in those six months had he felt as defenseless as he did now.

Because this wasn't a dream. It was his life and, true to form, Dom had once again lost someone very important to him. For a flash, an image of a beautiful young girl with wild corkscrew curls flashed in his head. Ruthlessly, Dom pushed it away, but then all he saw was Joel—dedicated cop, loyal friend, happier than he'd ever been.

"Dom? Did you hear what I said? Joel's dead." Cam's voice was pitched low but rubbed against Dom's skin like a jagged blade.

"When—?" was all that Dom managed to croak out.

"Around 3:00 a.m. He was—" Cam looked away, swallowing hard. "He was shot in the abdomen with his service weapon."

"His weapon? How's that—"

"There's talk of suicide."

The nasty word pounded into Dom's brain, obliterating the fog and replacing it with a wash of rage. Cam's blue-blood British accent held a trace of something Dom didn't miss— disdain. Dom growled and suddenly he had Cam pinned against his living room wall, his arm against the man's throat. "Take that back."

Although his features reflected the shock Dom felt, Cam didn't resist. Didn't fight him. He simply stared at Dom, his muscles relaxed, his eyes shadowed. "I didn't say I believe it," he whispered. "He was my friend, too, Dom."

Instantly, Dom lowered his arm and took three steps back.

"Look, we've reason to believe Mark Guapo was involved. That—"

At Cam's mention of Mark Guapo, a buzzing started in Dom's ears. Once again, his mind swept back to his conversation with Joel. Joel had been filling him in on the latest goings-on in the office—in Dom's undercover absence, one of their fellow detectives had gotten separated and another had just been served divorce papers—as well as the scoop on recently convicted drug lord, Mark Guapo. Prison, it seemed, wasn't keeping the man down. Last week, Guapo's men had thrown their boss's defense attorney off a twelve-story building. Lieutenant Masters was afraid the judge from Guapo's trial would be next…only Dom had sensed Joel holding something back. When he'd pushed, his friend had dropped several small bombs.

"Something's bothering me with his whole Guapo case," Joel had said last night. "I mean, the affidavit Manelli filled out for the warrant was tight. It laid out more than enough probable cause for us to search Guapo's place. But after Guapo's defense attorney was killed, I ran his phone records and noticed something. A phone call made to Judge Butler's chambers just hours before his estimated time of death."

"Judge Butler sentenced Guapo to prison. So what was it? A plea for help?" Dom asked.

"Or a warning. Judge Butler said it was simply a personal call—they're golf buddies—and there's no reason to think the judge is lying or hiding anything. But either way, someone on the inside might be able to tell us if the judge needs further protection or if he—or someone on his staff—is receiving information relevant to a murder. Plus, despite Guapo's conviction, his operation is as strong as ever. There's talk that he's expanding beyond drugs and stolen cars to firearms. That's why, if you continue to fight me on taking some time off, I want you to go undercover as Judge Butler's bailiff. Keep an eye out for anything suspicious. I've already talked to the lieutenant and he's on board."

Stroking his chin, Dom tried to ingest it all. "And the Sheriff's Department? How do they feel about Sac PD infiltrating their territory?"

"The Sheriff's Department knows you're coming, but only the heads know why. As far as everyone else is concerned, you'd be going in as who you are, a cop suffering from imminent burnout who needs a low-stress assignment for a month until we can figure out what to do with you."

It wasn't the first time Joel had insisted Dom take a break—but he sensed this was the first time Joel, now that he'd been promoted to being Dom's boss, was willing to follow through and make it happen. Pose as a bailiff or take some time off. For some reason, the latter held the most appeal. Maybe Joel was right. Maybe he could use some time to rest. To think. Lately, he'd been struggling against a strange sense of restlessness. An urge to dispense with the games and simply be himself.

Now why would he want something like that? He barely even knew who he was.

With the thought came a sudden cramping in his gut that had plagued him for the past week. His damn ulcer was acting up again. Refusing to rub it, refusing to acknowledge it, Dom gritted his teeth until it went away. A few seconds. Same as before. Which meant it was nothing. Just like his restlessness was nothing.

"Don't worry about the bailiff assignment being too boring for you," Joel interrupted his thoughts. "Danger seems to follow you no matter where you go. Plus, you can always hope someone recognizes you from a previous undercover op. That would certainly spice things up."

"Quit trying to make me feel better," Dom growled, playing along even though Joel's attempt at humor sounded strained. "No one would recognize me once I'm out of this getup." With his hair dyed black and the dark contacts, Dom could have passed for Joel's brother. Once he was close-shaven, with blond hair and blue eyes again, no one, not even his last lover, would recognize him. "So what are the chances I'll actually see action on this?"

"Slim to none," Joel admitted. "This is all speculation. Chances are you'll probably just be doing regular duty for the entire month."

Which was why, in the end, Dom had said he'd think about it—he hadn't been able to decide between bored and deathly bored, but working. Joel had handed him a stack of files and told him to look at them before they talked later today.

But he was never going to be able to talk to his friend again.

Just like with Mattie, the only woman Dom had ever loved, he'd have to settle for memories. Memories that were never enough to comfort, only to hurt. To remind him why loving others and being an undercover street cop was so damn dangerous—eventually, chances were someone ended up feeling exactly the way he was now.

He turned away from Cam, who was still talking. Dom blinked to stem the heat of tears in his eyes. The last thing Joel had said to him was how happy he was. How he hoped Dom would meet someone who made him as happy as Tawny made Joel. Dom had barely stopped himself from saying he'd had that kind of love once, only it hadn't lasted. That he'd given up the girl to ensure *her* happiness. That—oh no.

Swiftly, Dom turned back, interrupting Cam midsentence. "Tawny—?"

Had his friend suffered that indignity as well? Had he watched the fiery street reporter, the woman he loved more than anyone or anything, die before he met his own fate?

But Cam shook his head. "She wasn't hurt. She was out on an assignment. But she—" Cam winced and the broad, muscular man who was known for his cool under pressure suddenly looked ready to break. "She found him. She was the one to call 911."

Through sheer will, Dom walked to the couch and sat down, his head in his hands, his vision focused desperately on the beige carpet Joel had once given him grief about, telling him to add some color and vibrancy into his life.

Murder. Defense attorney. Guapo. Cam had said there was reason to think Guapo was involved in Joel's murder….

Dom sat up. "Guapo—"

Cam nodded. "When patrol arrived and swept the place, they found bundles of cocaine in the back of Joel's garage closet. Based on packaging, it matches the stuff recovered at the Guapo sting. Testing will confirm if it's from the same source." For a moment, Cam hesitated, then forced himself to continue. "Frank Manelli's M.I.A."

"Manelli?" The same man who'd served the search warrant with Joel? The one who'd just been served divorced papers? He struggled to make sense of Manelli's disappearance even as he tried to reason out why Joel would have had bundles of cocaine in his garage. "Has anyone talked to Manelli's wife, Grace?"

Cam's eyes flickered only briefly, a sure sign that in the six months Dom had been away, he hadn't managed to get over his feelings for Grace Manelli. "Lieutenant Masters called her right after Joel was found. She said Frank's been staying at a motel in Del Paso Heights. The motel manager said the last time he saw him was yesterday afternoon. There was no evidence of forced entry in his room. People are saying that he and Joel were on the take. That Frank wanted to sell the drugs they'd taken and shot Joel when he refused to go along."

"No." The word came out as a whisper, punctuated by a loud crash when Dom stood and kicked his coffee table over. Again, although the coffee table came within inches of Cam's legs, the taller man didn't flinch. "No! No way does anyone think that Joel was on the take. Frank, maybe. I didn't know him that well. But Joel? That's as stupid as thinking he would take his own life. He and Tawny were happy. He proved that a cop could—"

Biting off his next words, Dom clenched his fists. Joel hadn't proved anything except that Dom was right to avoid romantic entanglements, and now Tawny had to live with the tragic consequences. Dom paced. He tried to express himself, but couldn't, so he did the next best thing. He punched the wall, then did it again, confused when there was no pain as a result. No pain that could compete with the tight, gnawing despair in his chest.

Pressing his palms against the wall, leaning into it for support and hanging his head, he finally admitted what he'd been denying. A part of him had believed it was possible. That Joel—despite all odds to the contrary—would prove that a cop could have it all. The life and the wife. But now, before he'd had the chance, someone had taken not only his life and his happiness away—but was trying to take his reputation, too.

"I've gotta make a call, Cam."

Cam shifted uneasily. He didn't blame the guy. Dom, like Cam, had a rep for being unflappable. He wasn't prone to spurts of uncontrollable violence, not even on the job. Not even when other friends had died in the line of duty. In fact, it was during those times that he was the most restrained. He had an unnatural talent to freeze his emotions and stand apart from any chaos brewing around him. But this was different. This was Joel. Punching a wall seemed insignificant given the emotions still threatening to burst out of him.

"Do you want me to—?"

He shook his head. "I'll be fine."

"If you need anything—"

Dom closed his eyes. "Thanks."

When he heard the click of the door shutting, Dom stared at the phone. It took him almost twenty minutes before he had the strength to reach for it. Another twenty minutes before his body stopped shaking long enough for him to dial the number. The grief was pushing harder now to get out, chipping at the ice encasing his heart.

Not yet. Not yet. I can't fall apart yet.

First he had to correct a mistake he'd made and do what he should have done from the very beginning. Backed up his friend. He punched in Lieutenant Masters's number.

"Masters."

"Lieutenant, this is Dom Jeffries. The job with Judge Butler? I want it."

The lieutenant sighed. "Listen, son, I think you should take some time off. You've been in the field a long time. Joel thought so. And now, with what's happened—"

"Joel wanted me to take this assignment. I want it." Despite the grief threatening to burst through his chest and the fact his body still trembled, Dom's tone was implacable. It left no room for discussion about time off, Joel's death, or Dom's feelings.

No, not his death—his *murder*. Of all people, the lieutenant should understand the distraction Dom needed to keep from falling apart.

Sure enough, after a brief pause, the lieutenant said, "Let me get the files. You got copies?"

"They're right here." Ruthlessly, Dom moved toward the dining room and the files he'd dumped on the table. As he waited for the lieutenant to come back on the line, he flipped open the file documenting Guapo's arrest and conviction. First, he scanned the warrant. Then he checked the identity of the six officers who executed the search warrant. In addition to Manelli and Joel, Dom recognized two other names, but two names were new to him. The district attorney who'd tried and convicted Guapo, Linda Delaney, was relatively inexperienced and only on her second rotation on the felony team. The fact that she'd prosecuted Guapo either meant it had been a slam-dunk conviction or her superior had enormous faith in her.

Dom reached for the judge's file next. Judge Butler appeared to have a sterling reputation. Too clean, in fact. Without a hint of a single skeleton, it made Dom instantly suspicious. It also made him wonder if he used his staff to hide the bones that had to exist somewhere.

"All right, I've got them. What do you know?"

"I've looked over the Guapo file and the file on Judge Butler. I know you're friends with the judge and you believe he might be in danger." What he didn't reveal was Joel's suspicion that Judge Butler might be dirty. And he wouldn't reveal it. Not to anyone. Not until he found out whether it was true or not.

"Then let's go over the judge's staff files. There's the judge's clerk, Brenda Florentine. A law school intern. And his regular court reporter."

Dom took the files and opened up the first one. Brenda Florentine's picture was the first thing he saw. She was sexy in an overt way with a slight hardness in her eyes that immediately told Dom she was both experienced and probably street savvy. "What about the court reporter? Was she present during Guapo's trial?"

"Not sure, but does it matter? The defense attorney I can understand. Even the judge. But you don't think Guapo would go after the court reporter, do you?"

Dom opened the next file, and stared at the picture of a youthful blonde. She was definitely no more than early twenties. "If he's responsible for the defense attorney and Joel, why not?" Flipping the picture over, he read her security documents and confirmed she was the law student.

"Is that what this is about, Dom? Pinning Joel's murder on Guapo? The drugs—"

"Were planted. No way was Joel on the take. I know it. So do you, sir. That's why you made him sergeant."

"I'm hoping you're right, Dom. I'm sure hoping. Now, about the court reporter. She seems to have the closest relationship with the judge. She—"

Joel opened the final folder.

And felt the breath literally slam out of his body.

Stunned, he stared at the picture of a woman with corkscrew curls and big doe eyes, the same woman whose image had flashed in his mind when Cam had still been here. He felt an immediate tightening in his gut and lower. He knew it couldn't be true, but then again he'd already established he wasn't dreaming.

Apparently, however, his nightmare had just gotten worse. He'd just lost his best friend and now—

It was Mattie. His Mattie. The girl he'd loved and lost in college.

Correction. The girl he'd driven away in college.

She still had the pale complexion and cupid-bow lips that looked like they'd been injected with filler. Just as he had the first time he'd seen her on campus, she managed to come across as part milkmaid and part bachelor party stripper.

His Mattie, the woman who'd painted and sculpted and written poetry, had become a court reporter? It was a safe, practical job, he realized. Proving that, in the end, those things were more important to her than passion. That he'd been right to break things off with her when he had.

Acutely aware that the lieutenant had stopped talking on the other line, Joel forced himself to speak. "What about the court's regular bailiff?" he asked, even as he flipped through the pages of Mattie's file.

"Cleared and on leave for a month."

Dom barely heard what the lieutenant was saying as he read Mattie's employment application.

Mathilda Nolan. Thirty-two. Assigned as Judge Butler's court reporter over three years ago, after she'd put in several years in the general pool. The box next to "Marital Status" had been left blank, with neither "Single" or "Married" checked. However, her health benefits form listed one dependent—Jordan Nolan. Daughter. No husband, but maybe he simply carried his own insurance.

"Dom? Dom!"

Dom jerked and shook his head to clear it. "I'm sorry. What did you ask, Lieutenant?"

"I asked if you're sure you're up for this assignment. Despite—?"

Despite Joel's death. Despite the fact he'd just found out about it. But what else was he going to do? Listen to people talk of suicide and corruption in the same breath as they talked about his friend? No way. "I'm taking it."

"You're not a machine, Dom," the lieutenant said softly. "Don't you ever get tired of it? Want something more?"

It was the same question Joel had asked him the night before. And unlike the lieutenant, Dom knew Joel hadn't been talking in generalities. Joel had wanted something specific for him—something like he'd found with Tawny.

Last night, Dom had forced a smile to his lips. For a moment, he'd opened himself up to a fantasy of him and Mattie, married since college graduation. The fantasy wouldn't form. "I'm happy you found more with Tawny, Joel. Honest. But don't fool yourself. That kind of thing isn't for most cops. And it's certainly not for me."

"What thing?" Joel had countered. "Love?"

"And all the things that come with it. Confinement. Restriction." Causing the woman who loved you to worry that you wouldn't come back. When there was the real possibility that you wouldn't. "It works for you, that's great. But I'm not fit for management. I belong on the streets and in the action."

Whether it's where I want to be anymore or not, Dom thought.

When he finally answered the lieutenant, Dom closed his eyes but forced his voice to remain strong. "I just want to finish the last assignment Joel gave me, Lieutenant. Please... just let me do that."

"Okay, Jeffries. Make sure Judge Butler's courtroom is secure and keep me informed. Then you're taking some time off, whether you want to or not."

Dom hung up without arguing.

He no longer doubted he'd see action on this assignment. With Joel's murder and its apparent connection to Guapo, chances were high Judge Butler and his staff would soon be next. He'd make sure Judge Butler's courtroom was secure, but more important, he'd complete three tasks.

Find his friend's murderer.

Make sure the person regretted every second he'd taken of Joel's life.

And...

He picked up Mattie's file and stared at the woman he'd loved and still thought of nearly every day of his life.

He hadn't been able to keep Joel safe, but he was going to damn well make sure Mattie stayed that way. To do so, he'd kill Guapo himself if he had to.

Chapter 2

The following Monday

After surviving a surprise pregnancy, the death of a husband, and a brother with a drug problem, Mattie had thought she was shockproof against the whims of Fate; then she walked into Judge Butler's courtroom and saw Dominic. Fate obviously had a twisted sense of humor.

Despite the ten years that had filled out his face and frame, she knew him instantly. When he turned from shaking Brenda's hand and saw her, however, she couldn't say the same for him.

His blue eyes, identical to the pair she saw every morning and every night, were still the same shade of turquoise that made her think of white sand and warm island breezes. His face, however, betrayed neither memory nor guilt.

Disbelief overrode the joy that had ignited upon seeing him. He didn't remember her.

Could that be? Her daughter, *Dominic's* daughter, was nine years old. When she looked at her daughter, when she saw Dominic in her eyes, in her lanky frame, and in her mischievous wit, she tortured herself with "what ifs." What if Dominic had known about her? What if she'd fought harder to be with him?

Not once had "What if he didn't remember her?" entered the equation.

Obviously, it should have.

"Mattie!" Judge Butler exclaimed. "I was just introducing our new deputy to everyone. Come on over and say hello."

It wasn't as if his tan sheriff's uniform—so he'd fulfilled his dream of becoming a cop, after all—hadn't warned her, but she still felt her knees tremble. Dom was to be their substitute bailiff?

Even after hearing her first name, his face remained blank and emotionless. Anger loosened inside her, simmering and volatile, ready to explode at the least provocation. No, she wasn't as thin as she'd once been. Her hair was pulled back from her face, and years of worry and grief had lined her face in places that had once been smooth. But for him not to remember her? The tiny piece of her heart that had remained hollow all these years, yearning for him and the family they could have been, seemed to fill with lead. Instead of making her feel whole, the sudden heavy weight threatened to rip her heart out of her chest.

Turn around, she told herself. *Walk away and don't come back*. But that type of behavior would simply call attention to herself, and make him notice her and ask questions. Forcing herself to remain calm, she moved forward. She stopped within a few feet of him, once more blasted by memories she couldn't ignore. Flummoxed, she felt the pull toward him and desperately held out her hand as if it could shield her. "Welcome." Her tone implied otherwise. "I'm Mattie Nolan."

His warm hand engulfed hers, gave a short squeeze, then dropped it. "Nice to meet you," he said before turning away.

She stared at him. The anger simmering inside her flashed hot and violent. Nice to meet you?

They'd dated for two months before he'd unceremoniously dumped her and she got a "nice to meet you?" She'd been right not to tell him about the pregnancy, she thought bitterly. If he could forget her so easily, he didn't deserve someone as precious as Jordan.

He spoke to one of the courthouse's other bailiffs. Helpless not to, she took him in. The boy she remembered was completely gone. As rough as he'd been then, he might as well have been carved out of granite now. Despite the blond hair and blue eyes that should have given him the appearance of a surfer dude rather than a badass, he'd compensated with sheer bulk and attitude. He gave off a solemn "don't mess with me" vibe that would suit his position in the courtroom well.

The thought spurred her to walk swiftly out of the courtroom and into the back offices.

She was supposed to work with this man? The same man who'd tossed her aside, leaving her alone to discover she was pregnant with his child?

She shoved her purse into the small cabinet in the break room, then collapsed into a chair.

Be fair, a voice countered. He hadn't known about the baby when he'd left her.

It wouldn't have made a difference, she snapped back. The hot sting of tears nipped at her eyes and she fanned them.

Don't cry for that man, she ordered herself.

She and Jordan were fine. Better than fine.

Still…she couldn't help remembering the conversation she and Jordan had last night. The same conversation they had in one form or another at least once a week. The conversation about her wanting a father.

Last night, however, Jordan hadn't even tried to be subtle. She'd cut to the chase with one blunt statement.

"I miss having a dad."

The softly spoken words had come from the other room and caused Mattie's heart to lodge in her throat. Closing her eyes, she'd taken a deep breath and set aside the pen she'd been using to pay bills.

Although she waited, Jordan didn't speak again. Slowly, Mattie braced her palms against the kitchen table, pushed herself up, and walked into the living room.

Her nine-year-old daughter was sprawled on the couch, her small legs propped on the back and her head hanging off the edge of the seat cushions. "Tough day at school?" she asked.

Jordan turned her head to look at her. "Christy Means brought her dad in for show and tell. He wore a suit. And they went out for ice cream afterwards."

"Hmm." Mattie nodded, trying to figure out which of those three things required having a father the most. "I can come in for show and tell, sweetie. And we can definitely go for ice cream after. I'm not sure I'm up for wearing a suit and tie though." Sitting beside her daughter, she waggled her eyebrows.

Jordan giggled and flipped around until she was sitting upright. Apparently, however, she wasn't through. "It's not the same though. We can't toss a football. You don't know how. Or climb a mountain. You'd be too scared."

"You want to do those things?" The thought of Jordan losing her footing and tumbling down a mountain made her stomach queasy. The last time she'd checked, Jordan still played with Barbies.

Jordan picked at a nail. "Sometimes I want to. But I can't. 'Cause my dad's in Heaven." Standing, she walked toward the framed picture of John Nolan, who'd died when she was five. Picking it up, she stared at it. "Sometimes I wish I had two dads. That way, one could watch me from Heaven and one could still be here with me." She glanced at Mattie, who swiftly inhaled.

Because at that moment, Jordan looked so much like her father—her *real* father—it made her want to weep.

Maybe sensing her mood, Jordan put down the picture frame and threw herself into Mattie's arms. They hugged until Mattie pulled away and smoothed Jordan's hair from her face. "We can learn to throw a football and climb a mountain together, okay?"

Jordan nodded. "And go kayaking?" she asked.

Before Mattie could say more, the doorbell rang and Jordan's best friend, Lisa, asked her to play. With a swift kiss to Mattie's cheek and a promise to stay out of the street, Jordan was gone.

Now, after seeing the blankness is Dom's eyes, Mattie told herself that she and Jordan didn't need Dom or anyone else to be happy. Not to throw a football. Not to climb a mountain. And not for anything else either.

Retrieving her purse, she grabbed her cell phone and dialed the number of her friend, Linda Delaney. "I've decided to find a man," she announced when Linda picked up.

Linda snorted. "And what's brought on this sudden decision? Jordan bugging you for a father again?"

"You know, I miss having a man around the house, too. Someone to share the chores with. To bring in some extra money. To—"

"—have wild monkey sex with?" Linda drawled.

"Oh please," Mattie said, even as her head filled with memories again.

She'd enjoyed sex with John but she hadn't loved it. Not the way she'd loved it with Dom. Sometimes, when sleep lowered her defenses and let him inside, she still dreamed about it.

The way his muscles had bunched when he'd braced himself over her.

The smell of his skin. His taste. The feel of him inside her. Stretching her.

Becoming one with her.

And the way he'd hold her and talk to her afterwards. As if she was precious to him.

As if there was no place on earth he'd rather be than with her.

Wild monkey sex, indeed. She'd had it once, and more, and what had it gotten her in the end?

Jordan, she reminded herself. It had gotten her Jordan. And that was all that mattered.

"…my friend I was telling you about. He's handsome. Smart. Kind to kids. I'm telling you, he could be the answer to what you and Jordan both need, Mattie. So what do you say?"

Mattie shook her head, determined to push the past back where it belonged. "I'm sorry, Linda. Who are you talking about?"

"Ty Martinez. The new deputy D.A. in our office. The one who asked about you. Can I give him a green light to call you?"

Mattie swallowed, recalling the times she'd seen Ty Martinez in court.

He was attractive. Confident without being cocky. And sometimes Mattie caught him looking at her with a slight smile on his face.

And still he did nothing for her.

What was she? Frozen from the neck down?

All the better to protect your heart with, a voice inside her whispered.

"Mattie?"

Taking a deep breath, she spoke in a rush. "Yes. Tell your friend I'm interested, Linda."

Linda whooped and carried on so long that Mattie actually laughed. When they hung up, Mattie grabbed a pen and opened several drawers until she found a phone book. She flipped pages until she found the right one, then circled one listing, then another.

Annoyed that her hands were trembling, she dialed the first number anyway.

"Midtown Rock-n-Roll Gym," a deep voice answered.

She swallowed hard, then forced the words. "Hi, I'd like to take a climbing lesson for beginners."

"Great. When do you want to start?"

She glanced at the clock. "How about this afternoon?"

Only years of practice enabled Dominic to keep talking as if he didn't have a care in the world. His insides, however, were clenched so tight that the dull ache that sometimes plagued him was threatening to burn him from the inside out.

I shook her hand, he thought. All this time, and she felt and smelled exactly the same.

She also still revealed her emotions through her eyes.

When she'd thought he didn't remember her, something he'd deliberately fostered, she'd been pissed. But mainly she'd been hurt. And despite all the arguments he'd had with himself about keeping the past where it belonged, he'd almost caved.

With his mouth opening to do just that, he'd had no choice but to turn away, knowing that would hurt her pride even more. It was a testament to her low opinion of him, and probably men in general, that she could actually believe he'd forgotten her.

Within twenty minutes of meeting her, Brenda Florentine had already filled him in on the courtroom gossip. She'd seemed particularly focused on Mattie, and had told Dom how Mattie's husband had died young, leaving her alone with a daughter to raise, so busy that she didn't even have time to date. Even without that information, he would have known instantly that Mattie's life hadn't been an easy one.

Although she felt and smelled the same, she didn't look the same. She was still youthful and beautiful, but the spark of light that had radiated from her had dimmed so much it had all but disappeared. There was a stillness about her, a quiet acceptance, that put him on edge and made him want to rip apart whoever had hurt her, including himself.

He hadn't meant to contribute to her pain again, but pretending he didn't remember her had seemed the best course. Joel's funeral had been over the weekend and the only thing that had kept him upright was his vow to find Joel's killer. He was here to do a job and that meant he had to keep his emotions in check. Distance would be the best way of accomplishing that with Mattie. Her anger would be an even better way.

Tuning back to Deputy Pete Littlefield, who was rattling off about an escape attempt a few years ago, Dominic began making mental notes of his impressions. The first person to check out was Brenda. And Deputy Littlefield might be a pretty close second.

Unfortunately, once he'd seen her, Dominic couldn't keep his thoughts off Mattie. He wanted to see her again, away from work and when she didn't know he was watching. Moreover, even though it had been his idea to feign memory loss, he had the conflicting urge to shake her up. To see if she really was as different as she seemed.

Besides, it wasn't as if he needed an excuse. He was here

to check out the staff just as much as Judge Butler. He just needed to make sure checking out Mattie didn't become an obsession.

Chapter 3

Mattie stared up at the rock wall in front of her and barely stopped herself from wincing.

What on earth had she been thinking?

The young woman next to her was about half her age and half her size, but had a big smile and confident air about her. "You ready to get going, ma'am?"

Licking her lips, Mattie closed her eyes and took a deep breath. The words "Are you sure this is safe?" were on the tip of her tongue, but she forced them back since the girl had repeatedly assured her it was. Of course, Mattie couldn't just take her at her word. That was the whole reason she was here. She needed to test things out herself—several times—before she let Jordan anywhere near the rock climbing gym.

Grasping the nearest handhold, she fit her foot into a notch in the wall, grabbed onto another protrusion and pulled herself up. Surprised at how easy it was, she did it again. Then again. Until she was several feet off the ground and feeling a surge of accomplishment.

She kept going.

Her daughter wanted to climb mountains, so climb mountains she would, with or without a father.

An image of Dom flashed in her mind and one of her feet slipped. Gasping, she dug her fingers into their perches and hugged the wall. Heart pounding fast, she gulped in air and peeked down. She was only up about fifteen feet with plenty more to go and although part of her was tempted to stop, she clenched her teeth and moved on.

Her mind, however, was still on Dom and she couldn't help remembering that day ten years ago when she'd let her fear destroy everything.

He'd been her first lover, the first man she'd loved, the only man who'd ever made her feel equal parts jittery arousal and rock solid contentment. Even though he'd been several years older and light-years more experienced, she'd known from the moment she'd seen him he was meant to be hers.

They'd been together about two months. Cuddling in bed, enjoying a lazy day after her last college final, he'd been skimming his hand over her body and face, the contrast of the gentle pressure and the intense, possessive gleam in his eyes making her oblivious to anything else. Then he'd gotten the call—his acceptance into the police academy. Just like that, Mattie had felt her entire world collapsing.

"Wouldn't it be safer to be a lawyer?" she'd blurted out, trying to keep the panic from her voice but not quite succeeding. "Maybe a criminal prosecutor? They put the bad guys away, too, you know—without getting shot at."

The grin he'd sported since getting the phone call had immediately faded and his brows had furrowed, which had only made her panic escalate. "The suits can't put them away until they've been caught first, Mattie. I've wanted to join the academy for years. You said you were okay with that. What's changed?"

Licking her lips, she'd been unable to shake her head. "It's just, that kind of work…it's so dangerous."

He'd put his arms around her. Bent until his forehead touched hers and he could look straight into her eyes. "I love you, baby. You know that. More than I ever thought—"

She'd pulled away, wanting to believe what he was saying but unable to understand why he'd risk their future for a job. "Then don't go. Don't become a cop. Please."

He'd closed his eyes, obviously striving for patience. When he'd opened them, his expression was gentle yet resolute. "Plenty of cops have families…."

"Yeah, I know," she'd snapped. "And from what I've researched, plenty of them end up divorced or leaving their wives widowed. I don't want to end up like that. I don't want to end up hating each other."

As soon as the words came out, she'd wanted to take them back. She'd sensed it immediately—the sudden distance between them. That had been the moment everything had changed.

Only he'd surprised her. Hugged her. Told her he loved her again. Made her believe that everything would be okay.

The next day, he'd broken things off, telling her they were both too young. She'd never had another boyfriend, he'd explained, and she needed to see other people before committing to one man.

A week later, she'd found out she was pregnant. When she went to see him, he was out on a date with Penny Miller. She'd cried all the way home, certain he couldn't have loved her. Not the way she'd loved him. And she'd gone looking for someone who would.

When she met John Nolan, she'd believed he'd always put her first.

Only now John was dead and Dom was back in her life. Dom's sudden appearance had understandably sent her into a tailspin, but eventually she'd been able to relax a bit. They'd been in the courtroom together all day, but he hadn't spoken to her except in the most perfunctory manner. Not once had his gaze lingered on her or reflected recognition. He hadn't ventured near her, certainly nowhere remotely close to her personal space. It might have made her suspicious if he hadn't kept his distance from the rest of the staff, as well. He was professional but aloof, as if they were all just pawns in a game of chess—his to manipulate, save or sacrifice at will. Except for their past and a natural curiosity, he made it easy for her to ignore him.

If only she could stop thinking about him.

"You're doing great!" her personal cheerleader yelled up at her.

"Great," Mattie muttered even as her arms trembled with the effort to pull herself up to the next level. Right next to her, a little boy, probably no older than Jordan, scampered up the wall like a spider. He gave her a boost of confidence.

She pulled herself up, enjoying the challenge of finding the best combination of holds and steps. She covered more ground and still more ground. Until she was sweating and exhausted but feeling powerful, too.

Then she realized exactly how high she'd climbed.

"Holy—" She bit off the rest of the curse and jerked her gaze up until she was staring straight at the wall in front of her. The sounds of her breathing echoed loudly in her ears. Feeling her grip slipping, she whimpered.

"Jump off," she heard her spotter yell and immediately thought, *not a chance.*

"Oh God, oh God," she chanted, afraid to look down again. Feeling dizzy, she closed her eyes and rested her cheek against the wall. *This is why I don't do stuff like this*, she thought.

"Jump off."

"Push back."

"I've got you."

Several people were shouting up at her now. For one crazy second, she actually thought she heard Dom's voice.

It jerked her out of her paralysis.

"You're doing this for Jordan," she reminded herself. "What if Jordan was stuck up here? What would you have her do?"

Blowing out a breath, she imagined the situation and was suddenly enveloped by a sense of calm. She was strong again. She had to be. For her daughter.

Mentally, she recalled her spotter's instructions. When she reached the point where she wanted to stop, she was to give her the signal, kick off the wall, and fall back, letting her harness and the attached cable lower her to the ground.

Lowering her gaze, she found her spotter and gave her a thumbs-up. She nodded and shouted, "Go ahead." Somehow, Mattie managed to kick and let go at the same time. Barely stifling a moan, she hung suspended in air before being steadily lowered to the ground.

When she got there, she trembled with relief. Her spotter knelt down beside her. "So what do you think? Ready to do it again?"

The denial was almost out of her mouth before she pressed her lips together, effectively quashing it. She held up a finger. "Give me a few minutes, okay?"

"Sure. Just signal me when you're ready. I'll be right over there." She motioned to an area just to Mattie's left, where a much steeper and taller rock wall was set up for advanced climbers. Nodding weakly, Mattie watched the girl approach another female spotter, who excitedly gestured towards the top of the wall. Within seconds, a crowd gathered. Squinting her eyes, Mattie turned to see what everyone was so interested in. Her breath caught. Someone came to stand next to her.

"It's amazing the guy can climb at all with cajones that big." Despite the awe-tinged whisper of the stranger standing next to her, Mattie's gaze never strayed from the man climbing up the wall, which was alternately smooth or obstacled with layered protrusions. She certainly didn't respond to the colorful assessment of his bravery. Stupidity was more like it.

Unlike the climbers on her side of the room, he wasn't hooked up to a harness and cable. There was nothing to stop him should a single slip or lapse in focus send him falling to the ground below. Just bulging muscles and determination.

He was so controlled. So sure of himself. It made her wonder if he'd be that confident in bed. Somehow she knew he would be. That when he decided to bed a woman, he'd give his full attention to pleasuring her. If he didn't kill himself first.

She shook her head at her fanciful thoughts, equally annoyed and encouraged by them. She wasn't the type to fantasize about strange men, no matter how hot they were. But at least she'd managed to forget about Dom for a minute. She chose to see that as a good sign.

Then the man turned his head just enough for her to get a clear view of his face.

Disbelief came first, then a flood of anger.

It was *him*. Had he followed her? Was he mocking her, trying to make her believe he didn't remember her, then conveniently showing up at the same gym?

Bastard!

Turning away, she started throwing her things into her gym bag. She wasn't going to let him get away with this. Tomorrow morning, she'd tell him exactly what she thought of his juvenile games....

"Damn!" The man next to her muttered the word, causing Mattie's gaze to fly back to Dom. Her heartbeat skyrocketed out of control. His left leg had slipped out from under him, interrupting his reach for rock. He didn't flail or kick the way Mattie would have expected. Instead, he hung suspended in air, his only lifeline his right-handed grip on the small overhang.

Panic reared its ugly claws. The tornado swirled to life inside her, just like it had when they'd been together and she'd imagined him being gunned down on the job. Only now, instead of him lying in his own blood in an alley somewhere, she pictured Dom's body falling to the ground and breaking into a hundred pieces.

"Wait. He's okay. Look." The man next to her gripped her arm at the same time he spoke, and the human connection grounded her. She fought back her panic and focused again on Dom.

When he slowly pulled himself up the few inches necessary to gain a two-handed hold on the wall, she let out a shaky breath and her heartbeat slowed to normal. Dom began to climb again, and she was vaguely aware of the man walking away with a mumbled "crazy bastard."

She agreed. He was a crazy bastard. She'd been right to question his chosen career—clearly being a cop was nothing more than a way to satisfy his suicidal urges—and to keep Jordan from him. At least now, the only one he was endangering by his crazed carelessness was himself.

Sitting back on her haunches, she closed her eyes and let her head hang. What was she going to do now? Confront him? Bring her past crashing straight into her present? Swallowing hard, she thought of Jordan and how impressed she would have been seeing Dom climb that wall. Of course, she wouldn't think of the danger he'd been in or the danger in which he might thoughtlessly place others. He'd still be a hero in her eyes.

The stab of jealousy was unwarranted, but there nonetheless.

No, she wasn't going to confront Dom. She'd chalk this up to being a huge coincidence because it would serve *her* purposes. It would keep her and Jordan out of the past and firmly in the present, and it would also keep Dom out of their future.

She opened her eyes, but when she looked up, Dom was gone. Surprised, she looked around and immediately saw him walking toward her. He'd donned a ragged T-shirt and was swiping at his face with a white towel. He stopped beside her, making her crane her neck to see him.

"Ms. Nolan, right?" His voice was strong though slightly breathless.

Purposely keeping her expression blank, she nodded. "Yes."

"It must have been you who left the phone book in the break room open. I saw the ad for this place. I've been looking for another rock gym for awhile."

Sure, he had, but she was more than willing to let him play whatever game he was pursuing. Still, she couldn't stop herself from saying, "Why don't you just step in front of a car and get it over with? It would be quicker that way."

His expression didn't change, but his gaze flickered. He looked over his shoulder to where another man was starting to climb the same wall. Again, without a harness or cable. "There's a safety mat underneath the wall," he said softly. "You just can't see if from here."

With that, he left. Mortified, Mattie stared at the floor beneath her.

Okay, so he wasn't quite as foolhardy as she'd thought.

Didn't matter. He was still an adrenaline junkie and she didn't want anything to do with him. That went double for Jordan.

"How are you doing?"

She glanced up at her spotter, who looked as cheery as ever. She swiped an arm across her forehead and took a long gulp of water from her water bottle. Then she nodded, her expression grim. "Let's do it again."

Chapter 4

Wednesday

If unwanted fantasizing could kill a woman, then Dominic had likely lured many women to their graves. Despite her best efforts, and whether he knew it or not, he had Mattie's fantasies working overtime, taunting her with what she couldn't have.

What she didn't *want*, she corrected.

Unfortunately, Brenda was making it difficult for her to remember that.

For the past two days, it seemed no matter where Dom went, there Brenda was, throwing herself at him.

At lunch yesterday, Mattie had been sitting at the break room table nursing a Diet Coke when they'd walked in together. With every intention of leaving, she'd heard Brenda grilling him about his dating habits. Every muscle in her body had frozen and, curious in spite of herself, she'd listened as Dom tried to politely dodge the question.

Brenda had persisted, going so far as to say a "friend" of hers had bet her twenty bucks she couldn't find out the most unusual way a woman had tried to get Dom's interest. Mattie had been unable to stop herself from snorting and rolling her eyes.

Which, of course, had brought Dom's attention straight to her.

Cheeks turning cherry-red, she'd forced her gaze to stay on his and even managed to cock a brow. "Well, Deputy Jeffries, don't hesitate on my account," she'd goaded. "We wouldn't want Brenda to miss out on twenty bucks, now would we?"

Brenda had giggled and laid her hand on Dom's arm. Dom hadn't even looked at her. Instead, still staring at Mattie, he'd said, "Naked pictures."

Shocked at his answer—that he'd answer at all—Mattie's mouth had dropped open.

Brenda had slapped his arm. "Really? How'd she look?"

Her stomach rolling, Mattie had immediately dropped her gaze. Her knuckles had been white from where they gripped the edge of the table. Mortified, she could only listen to the rest of the conversation with dread.

After a brief hesitation, Dom answered quietly. "She looked...willing."

"No surprise," Brenda squealed.

When he didn't answer, Mattie glanced up again. He was looking at her.

Pain and jealousy had pricked at her like needles, angering her.

Aware that Brenda was now looking at her, too, Mattie had raised her chin. "Was she good?" she'd asked, wishing she had the nerve to dump her Coke on his head. Or, better yet, down Brenda's skintight sweater.

He'd shrugged. "She turned out to have a good heart, actually. But I never saw her again."

"Why not?" she'd practically sneered. "Did her 'good heart' intimidate you?"

His mouth had tipped up on one side in the barest hint of a smile. "No, but *my* heart wasn't in it. You see, I only wanted to be with one woman at the time. Things hadn't worked out for us, but I never forgot her. I guess once I'd been with her, not even a bold come-on and a good heart was going to cut it."

With a swift almost painful breath, she'd watched him walk away. Brenda had been right beside him.

Now, taking her seat in Judge Butler's courtroom for the morning calendar, her compact stenograph in front of her, Mattie staunchly refused to look at the tall man standing guard just behind her. Unfortunately, she didn't need to look at him to know that his short-sleeved, tan uniform hugged his muscular shoulders and thick thighs to perfection. Just like it had every day this week.

Hating the way her feelings and libido had gotten so out of control, she wanted to kick herself anytime desire made her stomach clench. In fairness, however, she'd be kicking herself all the time. Instead, she tried to concentrate on the routine of her job, her worries about Jordan, and her healing but fragile relationship with her brother, Tony. When that didn't work, she tried to drum up some excitement for her date with Ty that night. In the past week, the man had sent her flowers and called just to chat. He was intelligent, charming and clearly interested in her despite the fact she was a single mother. All she could think of, however, was Dom. Even after the incident in the break room yesterday, she'd pulled her box of college memorabilia out of the attic and spent hours looking at photos and reading his letters.

That made her a fool but, even worse, a masochist.

Yet, she couldn't deny it. Ever since Dominic had started working in Judge Butler's courtroom, his image had haunted her at all times of the day and night. Short, sun-kissed brown hair framing piercing blue eyes. Prominent, angular jaw. And the slightest hint of a cleft chin that made her lips tingle with the desire to kiss it.

One month, she told herself desperately. He was only here for one month until their regular bailiff returned from paternity leave. That was less than twenty workdays. Surely she could hold it together that long.

"Mattie, you've got a phone call on line three."

Glancing up, Mattie waved at the judge's perky intern, who immediately went back to texting her boyfriend. Thankful for the interruption lest she actually start salivating over the man behind her, Mattie picked up the phone. "This is Mathilda Nolan."

The voice that answered was phlegmy and studded with hoarse coughs. "Mattie…it's Jennifer."

"Jennifer Taylor?" she asked with a hint of dread. Sure enough, it was Jordan's after-school caregiver, calling to say she'd come down with pneumonia and that she'd have to close her program for at least a few days. Mattie hung up the phone and groaned.

She was barely making ends meet and couldn't afford to leave work early. The only person she knew who could pick up Jordan from school was Tony and he—

"Something wrong?" The deep voice startled her, but it was the sudden whiff of clean, male ruggedness that caused her to take a long, careful breath. Did Dominic have to smell as delicious as he looked?

Without turning around, she said, "No. Just a hitch with my daughter's day care."

"Your boyfriend can't pick her up?"

Mattie hesitated, unsure why he was angling for personal information. She shook her head and picked up the phone again. If Jordan stayed at school for tutoring, her brother

Tony could pick her up and bring her home. He'd only have to watch her for a couple of hours before Mattie got off. Then her regular babysitter would take over while Mattie went on her first date with Ty Martinez.

Mattie sighed and rubbed her temple, trying to rub away the frisson of doubt that poked at her. *It's okay,* she told herself. *You can trust Tony now. He's proven himself time and again.*

With a decisive nod, Mattie dialed Tony's number and made her request. Her brother instantly agreed and Mattie hung up the phone, proud that she'd given Tony the benefit of the doubt. Everyone deserved a second chance, didn't they?

Glancing at the clock, she started her finger exercises, well aware that today's calendar was going to be a busy one. Without the exercises, her fingers would ache so badly at the end of the day that she'd be in a bad mood for the rest of the night.

"A man might wonder exactly what you're training those fingers for, you know."

At the sound of her friend's joking voice, Mattie smiled and turned. Instantly, however, Mattie could tell something was wrong. Deputy D.A. Linda Delaney, a woman who prided herself on her ability to eat conflict for breakfast, had shadows under her eyes and no makeup on her normally cosmetically enhanced face. Mattie stood and rushed toward her. "What is it?"

Linda grimaced. "What gave me away?"

"Your lack of lipstick."

"That hideous?"

"Stop it, Ms. Argyle Teen Beauty Queen."

"I knew I should never have told you that. It'll always come back to haunt me."

"What happened? Did you get another phone call?"

Linda had gotten a few hang-ups over the last few months,

but hadn't seemed particularly concerned. Not until the calls had increased to five or ten a day. Then she'd changed her number.

"No more calls. My—my apartment was broken into last night."

"What?!" Mattie reached out and pulled her friend in for a hug. "Were you home? Were you hurt?"

Linda pulled back. "No and no. But the place was trashed. Considering I live in under a thousand square feet, that isn't a lot of trash, but they broke the crystal heart my grandmother gave me before she died. It's—" She visibly tried to stop herself from releasing the tears in her eyes. "It's got a huge crack in it now."

Mattie pulled her in for another hug and this time Linda squeezed back just as tight. "Oh, sweetie. I'm so sorry. Have you called the police?"

Sniffing but controlling her tears, Linda shot Mattie a tight smile. "Yes. They processed the place. Took a report. And they said—"

"Ladies."

Mattie jerked at the sound of Dominic's voice. He stood behind them, his face as impassive as ever. "Transport was running late but the in-custody defendants are finally here. I need to clear the courtroom."

"Give us a minute. Can't you see Linda is upset?"

Linda placed a hand on Mattie's arm. "It's okay, Mattie. I've got someone I need to talk to anyway." She jerked her thumb in the direction of the hallway. Through the window-paneled double doors, Mattie saw a uniformed officer.

"For a case or—" She glanced at Dom, unsure what he'd heard. "Or *your* case?"

"Mine."

"I hope he's good enough to find the lowlife responsible."

"That makes both of us. I'll stop by in a few hours. Lunch?"

Mattie nodded, but her friend had already turned and was headed out the door. Glancing at her watch, Mattie sighed. She should go back and tell Judge Butler the calendar would be ready to start soon, only she didn't want to dodge any more of his well-meaning questions about Tony. But Brenda had been on her cell phone off and on all morning, and the last time Mattie had seen her she'd been talking in hushed tones in a corner of the break room. That left her to get things started.

"Ms. Nolan?"

Once more, Mattie jerked at the low, masculine rumble behind her. She slowly turned to face Dominic, acutely aware of the betraying heat on her face. His normally composed features were now set in a slight frown of annoyance.

"Yes?"

"You need to leave, remember?"

He didn't smile. His eyes didn't crinkle at their edges. Somehow she still sensed his amusement. Feeling off-kilter, she glanced at the closed doorway of the in-custody holding area and then around the courtroom. They were alone.

Dominic stepped forward until he was just inches from her, close enough that she could feel the warmth emanating from his body. Automatically, she took two steps back, only to stumble on her chair. "Oh, no—" Her heartbeat accelerated rapidly as she felt herself falling.

Strong fingers closed around her arm and steadied her. She wobbled for a moment, then pushed her hair back from her face. Strong, yet gentle, she thought. He obviously still knew how to regulate that powerful body of his. "Thank you," she breathed. At least she'd fulfilled one fantasy—getting him to touch her again. And it felt far better than she'd have thought possible.

How pathetic was that?

Dominic said nothing, nor did he release her. Instead, they

stared at one another, their gazes locked. Heat warmed her skin from her head to her toes, settling into the nooks and crannies in between. She took a deep breath, trying to counter the sudden trembling in her limbs. For a split second, his gaze lowered to the rise of her chest. He dropped his hand and stepped back, his frown even more prominent than before.

"You're holding things up," he said abruptly.

The harshness of his tone registered like a slap. Straightening, she managed to glare at him. "I'm sorry for the inconvenience. Next time just let me fall." She bolstered her pride and stalked past him, heading for the narrow hallway between the courtroom, the interior offices, and Judge Butler's chambers.

Arrogant jerk. But this was great, she thought. Just what she needed. His bad attitude shook the fantasies right out of her. In fact, she just might—

Before she could complete the thought, the door to the in-custody room flew open, almost hitting her.

"No!"

She registered Dominic's yell just as a tall, thin-rail man dressed in an orange jumpsuit rushed into the courtroom. He froze in front of her, seeming as startled to see her as she was to see him. Behind him, another sheriff's deputy was wrestling with a second man in orange. The one in front lunged toward her.

She tried to scream, tried to dodge him, but she couldn't. Fear clogged her throat and all she could think was, *No, my family needs me.*

Even as she finally managed to turn, desperate fingers clawed at her arm. She screamed, pulling away, actually dragging the inmate forward two steps until he abruptly released her. Her own momentum carried her to the ground. The impact was hard enough to stun her, but she forced herself to scramble forward several feet before flipping onto her back.

She was just in time to see Dominic grab the man's arm, twist it behind his back, and shove him face first against one of the rectangular counsel tables. The inmate continued to struggle but Dominic effortlessly held him down. "Pete?" he shouted.

"I've got him," the other deputy called, his wheezing breaths clearly audible.

Dominic, on the other hand, seemed barely winded. His head snapped toward her. "Are you all right?" he barked.

Nodding frantically, she scooted back several more feet. His gaze ran over her, quick but thorough, narrowing when it settled on her arm. She looked down and saw several red, angry scratches where the inmate had grabbed her. He turned back to the inmate, who writhed and kicked out.

Bending down, he whispered something in the man's ear that made him still. The inmate twisted his neck, and shot Mattie a look filled with fear before he disguised it with a sneer and muffled curse.

After cuffing him, Dominic dragged him forward, stopping several feet from her. "Apologize to the lady, Dusty."

Glancing at the other inmate who was now sprawled face-down on the floor of the holding room, Dusty frowned and shrugged. "I'm not saying nothing—" He winced when Dominic grabbed his hair and pulled his head back.

"Apologize," he gritted.

"Really," Mattie said. "It's okay." *Just get him out of here,* she thought. *What are you waiting for?*

Both men ignored her.

"*Now*, Dusty. Or I can guarantee your trip back to jail isn't going to be as pleasant as the one that got you here." By the sound of Dominic's voice, he meant every word he said. The inmate wasn't willing to take his chances.

"I'm sorry," Dusty muttered.

"Ma'am. Call her ma'am."

The inmate swallowed audibly. "I'm sorry, ma'am."

"Mattie!"

Mattie glanced behind her. Brenda paused in the doorway as if she was too scared to come closer. The brightness of her neon-purple top and frosted pink lipstick seemed almost absurd given the situation.

Dominic propelled Dusty into the holding room, then reached for the door. "I need to secure these prisoners, but I'm calling backup. Brenda, please stay with Mattie." He looked back at her. "I'll be back in a second to speak with you and take care of those scratches."

"But I don't need—"

"It's standard procedure." He moved to close the door, then hesitated. "Are you sure you're okay?"

She stared at him, knowing something about him had changed but not sure what. "I'm okay."

Slowly, she got to her feet and backed up several steps toward Brenda.

With one last lingering look, Dominic shut the door. But not before she registered what was different. Before, he'd always looked calm. Controlled. The annoyance he'd shown before Dusty's appearance had been unusual enough. But just now… Lord, just now he'd looked primitive. Charged. Turned on. Not sexually, but by adrenaline.

It was a look she'd seen before. Ten years ago, whenever he'd talked about joining the police academy and working the streets, fighting crime like some comic-book superhero.

It was a look that made Mattie's stomach clench with both desire and dread.

Chapter 5

Picturing Mattie's stunned, pale face and the abrasions on her arm left his heart beating like a jackhammer. Dom shoved Dusty Monroe into a metal chair bolted to the floor of the holding room and shackled him to it. He then whirled on Pete, who was breathing heavily and sweating. Another deputy, who'd obviously responded to Pete's call for backup, nodded at Dom as he dragged the other inmate out of the room and slammed the door to the transport bay.

"What the—" Closing his eyes, Dom sucked in a deep breath and reminded himself they weren't alone. With a quick glance at Dusty, who averted his gaze, Dom motioned for Pete to join him in the corner of the room.

"What happened?"

The wash of emotions over Pete's face was unmistakable. First, he looked stunned. Then confused. Then belligerent. The other man, shorter than Dom by six inches but heavier by at least fifty pounds, mentally pulled up his pants while sticking out his chest. "Don't talk to me like I'm an idiot, Jeffries. I've been securing this courthouse for over five years now. I don't need some burned-out blue boy coming in here and copping an attitude with me."

Narrowing his eyes, Dom didn't bother sticking his chest out. Lowering his head, he got in Pete's face. "You lost control of a prisoner who broke into my courtroom and accosted a woman. I'm not going to ask you again. What happened?"

Pete swallowed, then seemed to deflate before Dom's eyes. "The other one said he had to use the bathroom," he grumbled.

Dom felt his brows pop into his hairline. "They were shackled together, Pete. Why didn't you wait for me before you unhooked their waist belts? That's procedure."

Pete's response was an almost juvenile shrug. "They were low-level security. We were already running late and Johnson's case was first on the calendar. He hadn't gotten to talk to his attorney yet. I figured it would speed things up if I unhooked them myself."

Or maybe it would get him brownie points with the wealthy man and his powerful attorney? When Dom remained silent, his disgust obvious, Pete spat, "I know, I know. It was stupid. But Johnson's attorney's a big shot and I figured he'd file a complaint or something. How was I supposed to know that one would run?" He shot a glare at Dusty.

"Did Johnson suggest you unhook him?"

The way Pete pressed his lips together told Dom all he needed to know.

"It was probably a setup from the beginning," Dom gritted. "They might have even delayed things at the jail themselves. Did you sweep the holding room before you brought them in? Do you know—"

"Look," Pete interrupted. "I don't answer to you, *Detective*.

I need to get this prisoner back to the jail and get some paperwork filled out."

Staring at the man who'd been more than civil to him in the past, Dom took a step back and crossed his arms over his chest. "I'm going to interview Dusty, but I need to check on the woman he attacked first. Watch him. When I get back, I'll call the jail when he's ready to be transported."

Shaking his head, Pete sputtered. "He's not going forward with the calendar, so he's going back."

Knowing he'd perfected it, Dom let a slow, menacing smile spread across his face. "Don't test me, Pete. He's staying so I can talk to him. You got a problem with that, you can take it up with your supervisor. Seems to me, though, that you have other things to worry about."

They stared at each other, neither one of them blinking. As Dom watched, Pete's face flushed a deep red, and the vein in his temple started to throb. "Fine."

Dom held his gaze for a few seconds longer, then turned to Dusty. "Try something again and you'll regret it, we clear?" Although the inmate didn't speak, Dom saw his agreement in his eyes. With a muttered curse, he called for backup, not caring how that would look to Pete. When another deputy arrived, Dom snapped, "Keep this inmate cuffed and contained until I get back."

Then Dom went in search of Mattie.

It didn't take him long to find her. She was in the staff break room, facing the sink with the water running, her back to him. He took a few seconds to regain his composure, but when he noticed her trembling, he immediately wanted to go back and pound Dusty into the ground. Instead, he stepped forward with a soft, "Let me take a look at your arm."

Gasping, she whirled around, her forearm dripping. Her eyes were wide, her face pale. When she spoke, her teeth were chattering, "I'm fine. I—I told you, I don't need—"

Moving slow so he wouldn't scare her even more, he reached around her to turn off the water. He gently lifted her arm to inspect it and asked, "Why are you in here alone?" to distract her.

"I told them I was fine and to stop hovering. Court should be starting soon."

"Hmm." Gently, he smoothed his fingers over the red welts on her arm, noting that one mark had drawn blood and several bruises were also starting to form. She was right. She seemed fine, but Dusty was a druggie and a transient. Who knew what he was carrying.

Barring that, she'd been lucky. Inmates manufactured shanks all the time. If Dusty had managed to slip one in with him—

"Where's the inmate?" she asked even as she pulled away.

Dom clenched his jaw and barely resisted the urge to grab for her. He forced himself to take several steps back. "He's in the holding cell. Don't worry, I have another guard watching him, one who isn't a damn fool this time."

She nodded. Looked over his shoulder. "Good. That's... good."

When he didn't speak or move away, she gestured to the door. "Well, I need to get the—"

Unable to help himself, he raised his hand and hooked a strand of her hair that had fallen in her eyes. Despite her quick inhalation of breath, he tucked it behind her ear and let his hand hover there. Their gazes locked and he felt his heart slam against his chest, over and over, beating into his brain, *It's her, It's her, It's her.*

Her lips parted and she moistened them with her tongue. Helpless, his gaze followed the movement and lingered. This close to her, his body shifted into autopilot, as if ten years had never passed. He grew aroused. His breath deepened.

His fingers itched to reacquaint themselves with her hair and breasts and hips.

"Dom…?" she whispered. It had the effect of a gunshot.

Dropping his hand, he swiftly moved back, putting several feet between them. What the hell was wrong with him? He'd meant only to check up on her, yet the minute he got anywhere close to her, he lost his mind. She was certainly staring at him as if she believed that to be true.

"I'm going to need you to fill out a statement. Since I was a witness, I can't take it myself, so I'll send another deputy over. Please wait here."

"But I—"

Turning away, he pretended he didn't hear her.

He knew exactly what that made him.

An even bigger coward than when he'd broken up with her.

Mattie's knees were trembling so much she barely made it to a chair before she collapsed. Although she'd been shaken by the incident with the inmate, most of her current distress had to do with the man who'd just left—the same man who'd looked as if wanted to suck on her from head to toe. What was even worse, his intense scrutiny had made her own libido, put on ice for far too long now, go into overdrive. She felt flushed. Achy.

Empty.

But also confused.

Dom had looked at her with such tenderness. It seemed she was right. He *did* remember her. So why was he continuing to pretend he didn't?

A thought occurred to her and her chest constricted with shame.

Maybe he was worried she'd try to pick up where they'd left off. Maybe he figured, now that she was a single mother and getting on in years, never mind packing on a few extra pounds, she'd hit on him? But then why show so much concern for her arm? And what about the desire that had darkened his blue eyes?

Shaking her head, she closed her own eyes and took a deep breath. The man was as confusing as ever. And, she reminded herself, opening her eyes, she had better things to do than let him play with her emotions again. She'd fallen for that white knight, your-soul-calls-to-mine act before only to be dumped. Hard.

She needed to stay on course—protect herself and stay away from him.

Biting her lip, she retrieved her cell phone from her pocket and dialed Ty Martinez's number. "Hey, Ty. This is Mattie. I just wanted to say hello and tell you how much I'm looking forward to our date tonight."

"Idiot," Dom muttered as he made his way back to the in-custody holding cell. What had he been thinking? He should have known that with Mattie, even the slightest touch would send him over the edge. Now he couldn't get the dazed, heated look in her eyes out of his head. Despite their past, despite her believing he'd forgotten her, she'd responded just as violently to his closeness as he had. When she'd whispered his name, it had taken all his self-discipline to leave her rather than fall to his knees and confess everything—how much he'd missed her and still wanted her.

Only one thing had stopped him. As much as he wanted her, he wanted her safe most of all. To insure that, he needed to stay objective. He also needed to find out if Dusty had any connection to Guapo.

Reaching his destination, he paused, took a deep breath, and went inside. Pete was gone. He thanked the remaining deputy, then shut the door. The room was quiet except for Dusty's rough breathing. Deliberately, Dom remained silent for several more minutes before he turned and strode to the opposite side of the room. Grabbing an empty chair, he twirled it around and lowered himself into it. Straddling the chair and resting his chin on his folded arms, Dom stared at Dusty, noting how the usually easygoing inmate couldn't quite look him in the eye.

Minutes ticked by, but still Dom waited. When Dusty wasn't looking at the floor, he cast apprehensive glances at the door that led to the jail transport bay. The more time that passed, the more jittery Dusty became. He bounced his knee. Swiped his nose against his shoulder. Tossed his head like he had a permanent crick in his neck that he couldn't get rid of.

Despite the fact that the guy had been incarcerated for several weeks, his glassy, dilated eyes told Dom he was on something, most likely meth. That posed three immediate questions. Where'd he get it? Did he get it in exchange for making an attempt on Judge Butler? And was his ensuing assault upon Mattie coincidence?

Of course, it appeared coincidental. After all, if Dusty had arrived at the courthouse twenty minutes earlier, he would have been locked down well before Mattie ever stepped into the courtroom. But Dom didn't take anything at face value. Everything—the tardiness of the jail bus, Pete Littlefield's uncharacteristic carelessness, even Mattie herself—was immediately suspect.

It was another five minutes before Dusty snapped.

"Come on, man. You taking me into court or back to jail?"

Dom let him sweat another thirty seconds before answering. "Maybe neither."

The quiet words brought Dusty's gaze zooming directly to his. "Whad'ya mean?"

Straightening, he casually moved the chair he'd been sitting on against one wall and stepped closer. He loomed over

Dusty, forcing him to crane his neck up at him. "I mean, you made a mistake trying to hurt a woman on my watch, Dusty. Before, you were just a two-bit thief with a drug habit and a big mouth. Now, you're an attempted murderer."

Eyeballs practically popping out of their sockets, Dusty once more swiped his nose on the shoulder of his jumpsuit. "Murder? Yeah, right. I barely touched her."

"And exactly what were you planning on doing if you caught her? I bet you would have touched her a whole lot more."

Dusty grinned, showing several gaps between crooked, stained teeth. "It ain't like that, man. I just panicked. I've been in that little cell for days. I was starting to get claustrophobic."

Grasping the back of the other man's chair, Dom leaned down until he could see his reflection in Dusty's dark pupils. "Cut the bull. You're a small-time druggie, Dusty. You would have pled and been on your way to rehab in the next day or two. You've been in the system long enough to know that. So why'd you do it?"

"I told you, I panicked—"

Straightening, Dom forced himself to take a step back. Then another. That conflicting mix of ice and heat, the one he'd felt when Cam had told him about Joel, was back. He suddenly didn't trust himself not to step over the line, and his tenuous hold on his control shocked him. "The guy who gave you a fix. When did he first contact you?"

Dusty's gaze skittered away. "I don't know what you're talking about."

"You're going to take a drug test whether you want to or not, and then you're going to be charged with yet another count of under the influence. That, with a charge of assault and attempted escape? Well, let's just say you better get over that claustrophobia really fast. There won't be any more drug rehab on the horizon. You're going to prison, man. I can't see a skinny guy like you lasting very long there."

Dusty narrowed his eyes and spat on the floor. "I can handle it."

After staring at the blob of saliva on the floor, Dom looked back at Dusty. Fear flashed in the other man's eyes, making Dom smile evilly. He activated his radio. "Prisoner ready for transport back to the jail." Dom casually strolled toward the inner door that would take him back to the courtroom.

"Wait!"

He paused with his hand on the doorknob and slowly turned around. "Something you needed, Dusty?"

"So—um. So what happens if I tell you who gave me the stuff? You gonna drop the charges? You know, the assault. The escape charge?"

"I'm a cop, not a lawyer. I can't do anything like that. But if you cooperate, I'll talk to the D.A. myself. If you don't, well…"

Dusty swallowed hard and cast another glance at the outer door. "The other inmate. Martin Johnson. He slipped me a hit in the holding cell just before we loaded. Told me he had more and all I had to do was cause a little ruckus here."

Dom pressed the button on his radio. "Hold off on transport." He retraced his steps into the room. "Did he specify what kind of ruckus?"

"No."

"Did he say anything about the judge? Or Mathilda Nolan?"

"Who's Mathilda?" Realization sparked in his eyes. "Oh. The brown-haired babe?" Flicking his tongue obscenely, Dusty murmured, "You got something going with her?"

Dom was sure he didn't react by so much as a flicker, but Dusty latched onto the idea and wouldn't let go. "You do, don't you? Isn't that some kind of, I don't know, conflict or something?"

"Stay focused here. So for a hit of meth, you put your freedom on the line? With no further instruction than that? Without asking for any kind of motive?"

A shadow darkened Dusty's eyes before he narrowed them and snorted. "Freedom? I ain't been free for over twenty years, man. You ever been addicted? You ever needed something so bad, you were willing to do anything to get it?"

An image of Mattie's doe eyes and full lips flashed in Dom's mind before he ruthlessly shoved it away. He'd fought that particular craving for days, and just as he'd expected, it was Mattie and not sheer boredom that was making this assignment so tough.

"What do you know about Johnson?" Dom would get the man's file himself and talk to Pete after he debriefed Johnson. But it was always helpful to hear what the other inmates knew about one another.

Dusty snorted. "He ain't exactly forthcoming about himself, if you get my point."

Sighing, Dom shook his head. "Dusty, Dusty, Dusty. My willingness to help you with the D.A. is growing smaller as we speak. I know you've got ears. And I know you wouldn't pull something like this unless more than meth was involved. He threaten you?"

"No."

"Dusty."

Dusty's expression hardened. "He didn't threaten me, man. He just…he's got money. Pull. Resources, if you get my drift. How often does a Richie Rich land in the jail, willing to make my time a little easier in exchange for something so easy. I'm telling you, that's it. And I'm not saying anything else until my attorney gets here."

"Oh, that's fine." Dom leaned down close so that Dusty

was forced to look at him. The other man's eyes flickered with fear, which is exactly what Dom intended. "While you wait for your attorney, be sure to think about me. Because if you hurt that woman you attacked, if you ever come near her again, no one, not your attorney, not Mr. Richie Rich, not even your mother, will keep you safe."

Chapter 6

An hour later, Mattie thanked the sheriff's deputy who took her statement and the paramedic who'd come to examine her. When she'd asked who'd called the paramedics, the deputy had told her Dom. Talk about overkill. Although the paramedic had offered to take her to the hospital, she'd refused, just barely able to stop herself from rolling her eyes. Take her to the hospital for what? A few marks on her arm? With the courtroom packed with impatient attorneys and their clients, she knocked on Judge Butler's door.

"Come in," he called from inside.

Mattie opened the door and stepped into the judge's large, airy office. Judge Patrick Butler had graying hair and was of average height, but his lean frame could have belonged to someone fifteen years younger. He rose from behind his desk and waved her in. Mattie stepped inside but froze when she saw the much larger form rising from one of the plush chairs situated in front of the judge.

Dominic.

A slight frown furrowed his brows when he saw her. The nerves that had just started to calm within her tingled with awareness.

Focusing on the judge, Mattie said, "I'm done giving my statement, your honor. We can start court whenever you're ready."

"You told me you weren't hurt, Mattie, but Deputy Jeffries thinks you should be going to the hospital."

Refusing to look at the man whose gaze she could feel lasering into her, Mattie shook her head. "Deputy Jeffries is being overly cautious."

"Take off your sweater," the man in question ordered.

Mattie glared at him and clutched the black sweater she'd donned minutes before as if he meant to rip it off her.

He turned back to the judge. "Her right arm is scratched. With Dusty Monroe's background, I wouldn't take that lightly."

"I'm not asking you to take anything lightly," Mattie retorted. "I'm not asking you for anything at all. I'm fine. I washed the scratches and the paramedics checked me out. I'd really just like to get back to work now. The courtroom is packed and people are getting restless."

Mattie paused, fully aware she was babbling. Embarrassment and frustration made her snap, "Shouldn't you be out there doing your job instead of playing amateur doctor? You're only here for another few weeks, right?"

His frown deepened, then relaxed. His eyes took on a calculating air that made her automatically take a step back. One he noticed. "She's right, your honor. I'll relieve the deputy inside—"

Mattie flushed when she realized someone else had been watching the courtroom while he'd been talking to the judge.

"—and Pete can talk to you as soon as he's done at the station."

"Very well. Thank you, Deputy."

Dominic walked toward the door but paused by Mattie's side. "Who told you I was only here for a few weeks?"

Feigning a sudden interest in the judge's cream and blue striped curtains, Mattie shrugged and tried to sound unconcerned. "Our regular bailiff comes back from paternity leave at the end of the month." When he didn't answer immediately, she couldn't stop herself from looking up at him.

"That may be true, but I stay for as long as I'm needed."

Her jaw dropped at his words, stated so calmly but with an undeniable air of challenge. She knew for a fact he was lying. Tilting her chin up, she met his gaze squarely. "I don't need anything from you, Deputy Jeffries." Not anymore.

It was there again, that strange glimpse of amusement when his expression was entirely passive. He lowered his head to hers, his warm breath tickling her ear as he whispered, "Now, that hasn't always been true, has it, Mattie-mine?"

She reared back, staring at him as realization grabbed her by the throat and shook her like a rag doll. He did remember her. Any vindication or salve to her ego was overshadowed by suspicion, and the express confirmation that he'd been playing her for a fool and obviously felt no remorse.

She wasn't aware that her mouth had fallen open until he nudged it closed with one finger.

"Did you really think I wouldn't remember you the instant I saw you?" he said softly. "Or did you just pretend that's what you believed because it was the safest course?"

With that final question, he strode from the room, quietly shutting the door behind him.

She was still staring at the door when Judge Butler chuckled. "Something you want to tell me, Mattie?"

Startled, she shook her head. "What? Of course not, your honor. Deputy Jeffries is just being overly—"

"—cautious. Yes, so you said. Are you sure you're okay?"

"Yes, I'm fine." Now there was a whopper of a lie. Dominic's challenge—and that's certainly what it had been—had her knees knocking together under her skirt. "Thank you, your honor."

Mattie walked to the door and pulled it open just as the judge called to her. She turned with her hand on the doorknob.

"Yes?"

"I'm glad you weren't hurt today, Mattie." He rose, placed a gentle hand on her shoulder and squeezed. Uncomfortable with the intensity of his gaze, she stepped away when his touch lingered. He noted her movement, but smiled anyway. "How is Tony doing? You know I'm always here if either of you need me, but I haven't heard from him in awhile."

With a smile that hopefully reflected her appreciation, Mattie responded, "Tony's fine. Thank you for asking."

Raising his arm, Judge Butler showed her the small shopping bag in his hand. He smiled sheepishly. "You know what good friends your parents were to me. Margaret and I wanted to give you a few things. I know times are tough for you now." He raised his hand to forestall Mattie's protest. "Nothing lavish. Just a few small gifts for you and Jordan. Tony, too. Would you give it to him?"

"Of course." Mattie took the bag he offered. "Thank you again." Stepping outside, she shut the door, then leaned back against it. She felt strange about the gifts and sincerely hoped they weren't anything expensive. If they were, she'd give them back. She'd always enjoyed and cherished her relationship with Judge Butler, but lately, something about his interest in her personal life made her uncomfortable. Closing her eyes, she took several slow, deep breaths. Weariness made her limbs heavy. Maybe Dominic had been right. Maybe she should have gone to the hospital, then home.

"Tough times, Mattie? That wasn't what I wanted for you at all."

Mattie's eyes popped open. Dominic was leaning against the opposite wall, his arms, muscular biceps bulging, crossed over his chest. Mattie straightened and cleared her throat, her composure quickly eluding her now that she knew he remembered her. Her body. The things they'd done and said to one another. The dreams she'd foolishly harbored.

Pasting a look of resigned boredom on her face, she replied, "No, what you wanted was for me to date other people. Of course, that was only so you could date other people. Penny Miller, wasn't that her name?"

His eyes narrowed. "You were the only girl I wanted, Mattie."

She stared at him, then burst out laughing as she shook her head. When her laughter bordered on the hysterical, she tried walking past him.

He blocked her, his face as impassive as ever. "There's something funny about that?"

Tilting her head, she studied him. He'd always been good at hiding his feelings. Even when they'd been as intimate as two people could be, she'd had a hard time reading him. She'd known it was because he hadn't wanted to be read. Still, when Dusty had attacked her in court, Dom hadn't been able to hide his reaction. He'd been pumped and angry, but he'd also been scared for her. He'd been worried when he'd found her in the break room, too. Without her wanting it to, that realization softened her anger. "I'm just thinking what a really odd day this is, and not," she added, "because I was almost assaulted by an inmate. And not because an old boyfriend has suddenly remembered who I am."

Referring to him as her boyfriend must have stunned him,

because she was able to walk around him. She'd only gone a few feet before he caught her elbow, stopping her. "Not almost assaulted. You were assaulted."

Eyes narrowed, she pulled away from him. Despite the scare Dusty had given them, Dom had no say in how she chose to describe the incident or what she did about it. "I'm fine."

"Right. And I told you, Mattie, I knew who you were instantly. I just pretended I didn't because I was trying to make things easier for you."

She had a fairly even temperament, she truly did, but Dominic was making her emotions bounce from one extreme to the other. He'd made it quite clear what he thought of her ten years ago. Granted, she'd probably speeded his rejection along, but she'd been scared. She'd wanted him safe, even if that meant giving up his dream job. After all, she'd thought she was his dream, too. Obviously not, since he'd certainly dropped her quick enough when things had started to get complicated. "You shouldn't have bothered. Seeing you again means absolutely nothing to me, Dominic. Less than nothing."

Even as the last words tripped off her tongue, she wondered how wise it was to challenge him. The way he clenched his jaw told her that a change of subject would probably be a good idea.

Eyes narrowing, he placed his hands on his hips, and looked her up and down. "Tell me something, Mattie, were you afraid of Dusty?"

Automatically, she stiffened. "So what if I was? Does that make me a coward?"

"No, but fear can be distracting. It can make you tune out everything but your own survival. Did he say anything to you?"

"In the three seconds before you caught him? Of course not. And why would he say anything to me?"

"Anything he said could be useful. It might tell us if he was going for a hostage, or if his goal was to break out or to break in."

"Break in?" She shook her head, confused. Why would an inmate break into the very courtroom he was already scheduled to appear in? This day was going from weird to weirder, and all she wanted was to go back to ignoring Dom—and have him to do the same. She still might fantasize, but fantasies, unlike her riotous emotions, could be hidden and contained. "Look, you're wasting my time. Can I go?"

"Sure." But he didn't move. Instead, he crossed his arms over his chest again and continued to block her path. A hint of a smile curved his lips. "You know, I guess one good thing came from Dusty's sudden appearance this morning." When she flexed her brows, he explained, "You're not afraid of me anymore."

The man's gall was so unbelievable. "I was never afraid of you." Afraid of the feelings he inspired, sure, but not of him.

The barely-there smile suddenly radiated pure arrogance. "Prove it. Have dinner with me."

"Dinner?" she sputtered. He'd gone from ignoring her to challenging her to questioning her, and now he was moving on to flirting with her? She reacted the way she always did when she felt threatened—on the offensive. "Are you crazy? I can't even stand the sight of you."

He didn't so much as lift an eyebrow, but his look turned reproachful. "You never used to lie."

"Too bad I can't say the same for you," she shot back.

"I never lied to you, Mattie."

She flushed, twisted her hands together, and wished she'd kept her mouth shut. It was true. He hadn't lied to her, but now that she'd given herself the freedom to speak her mind, she couldn't seem to stop. "Not by express words, no. But you know what they say—actions speak louder than words." And he'd acted plenty ten years ago. Boy, had he acted. Every touch, every kiss, had made her acutely aware of what she'd been missing before they'd made love. Not only the physical sensations of sexual desire, but the feeling of being cherished. Of being made to feel she was special to him. She'd grieved that loss for a long time, even after she'd met and married John.

"Then let's act," he insisted. "Have dinner with me. We can catch up. Put the past behind us."

Inside, she was stunned. Shattered. He was offering her the closure she'd never really gotten before. It was tempting, the idea of being able to forgive and forget. It's what would be healthy, wouldn't it? Outwardly, she called upon ten years of learning to live without him in order to appear unaffected. Hands on her hips, she tipped her head to the side, studying him. "I'm fine with keeping the past where it is. And why all this sudden interest? You haven't said one word to me that didn't have to do with my job." Well, besides the talk about naked pictures, of course, but she wasn't about to bring that up.

"You know more than anyone that I'm not overly talk-ative."

She smiled tightly. "No, unless it comes to making false promises." She held up her hand to forestall him speaking. "I know, I know. You never made false promises. The talk of driving cross-country and wraparound porches and baby quilts was all in my head. But at least you got what you wanted most. You became a cop."

His eyes darkened with some emotion she couldn't name. "I became a cop, yes. But you didn't imagine all the other stuff, Mattie. It was something I dreamed of, too. I was just realistic enough to know I couldn't have it." He stepped closer until she had to tilt her chin to look up at him. "Will you have dinner with me?" To her dismay, she was considering it. Desperately, she glanced around, trying to focus on her surroundings instead of the man in front of her. Unfortunately, the sparsely decorated hallway, with only a framed copy of the Declaration of Independence hanging off-kilter on one wall, couldn't compete with the man in front of her. Life, liberty and the pursuit of happiness, she thought. Such simply stated goals. She had her happiness. She had Jordan. Her brother, Tony. They had each other. She didn't need more. Or anyone else.

Her body shouted in protest, forcing her to recall the pleasure he'd always brought her. Not just physical, but emotional. A kind of sweet joy that she felt only one other time—when she looked at their daughter.

The daughter he could never know about. She might want closure and Jordan might need a father, but the stakes were too high. Instinctively, she knew Dominic wasn't a man who would take kindly to his own child being taken from him, even if he had abandoned her mother. What would stop him from trying to punish her by taking Jordan from her completely? Besides, her concerns about his profession were still valid—why let Jordan open her heart to someone who might end up leaving her, willingly or not?

But then again, Dom *was* her father.

Fighting her uncertainty, she tried to focus on the purple carpeting underfoot, but the size-12 boots next to her strappy black sandals were what she noticed. Her toes, recently painted a pale pink, peeked up at her and the contrast of her femininity and his unmistakable masculinity made her shiver.

Fear gave her the resolve she needed. "No, I don't want to have dinner with you," she responded. "And I'd appreciate it if you would just leave me alone."

He stared at her while heat climbed her face. Cursing her fair skin and its tendency to blush at the slightest provocation, she clenched her long skirt to keep from fidgeting. A noise behind them made her jump and glance back. Judge Butler paused in his doorway, his features twisted into an expression of annoyance.

"Shouldn't we have gotten started by now?" he questioned, his words clipped.

"Yes, your honor." Thankful for the interruption despite Judge Butler's annoyance, she rushed past Dominic and into the crowded courtroom. She signaled Brenda that the judge was coming in. In her periphery, she saw Dominic stride to the deputy standing guard next to the jury box and dismiss him.

From the courtroom audience, Linda waggled her brows and rolled her eyes in a mock swoon. She was teasing her about Dominic again. Weakly, Mattie waved, sat, and adjusted her skirt, trying to act normal. She moved her stenograph closer to her, tucked back her hair and licked her lips. She adjusted her skirt again. Twice. Then, unable to help herself, she casually lifted her gaze to peek at Dominic.

She gasped.

He was staring at her, his blue eyes darkened with an unmistakable heat that seemed to touch every part of her at once. Instantaneously, she felt exposed. Raw. Vulnerable. Her breathing quickened and a shiver of something frightening—anticipation? Excitement?—ran through her.

He lifted his eyebrows, as if he was asking her the question again. *Will you have dinner with me?*

In self-defense, she straightened and narrowed her eyes. "No," she mouthed, refusing to look away from his gaze.

But then her mouth dropped open and she nearly fell off her chair.

Because Dominic did something he hadn't done in ten years. At least, not in her presence.

He smiled. A huge smile that flashed strong white teeth and dimples, and transformed him into the hunky, handsome man she'd crushed on for weeks before she'd gathered the courage to approach him.

And then he winked at her.

Chapter 7

The rest of the day was uneventful, with the arraignment calendar flowing into two preliminary hearings, afternoon jury selection, and finally a suppression hearing. Nonetheless, Mattie's awareness of Dominic had grown ten-fold, until everything seemed to be about him and her and an invisible thread of sexual tension that tied them together. By the time the judge pronounced they were done for the day, Mattie's fingers were trembling and she couldn't get out of the courtroom fast enough.

She hastily covered up her stenograph and grabbed her files.

"Okay, you've got to fill me in. What the heck happened this morning?"

Linda walked through the swinging half doors that divided the court staff from the audience. A quick glance confirmed that Dominic was still at his post, his face impassive but focused on the two of them.

Clearing her throat, Mattie placed her free hand on Linda's back and steered her toward the door. "I don't know what you mean."

Linda, however, wouldn't cooperate. She stopped in the aisle and threw a curious glance at Dominic. "Uh, in case you missed it, lovey, you've got an admirer and it looks like he's not willing to be ignored anymore."

"Will you please lower your voice and stop looking at him?"

Linda just grinned. "After that last witness was excused, I thought he was going to rip your clothes off right there and then. Should I have stayed away and let him?"

"Be serious."

"I'm being completely serious. Now, tell me what happened this morning. Did you guys do it in the judge's chambers?"

Mattie juggled her files and slipped past Linda, who followed her out of the courtroom. She didn't stop until she was outside on the courthouse steps, breathing in air like she was starved for it. She wanted to spill her guts and tell Linda everything, but somehow she knew that if she actually verbalized her past and emotions about Dominic, she'd no longer be able to keep them at arm's length. It was already hurting her. She couldn't let it have a stronger hold than it already did.

"Whoa. Mattie?" Linda placed a hand on her shoulder, her pale green eyes shadowed with concern. "I'm just messing with you. Don't be mad."

Mattie nodded and put a hand over hers. "It's not you. I was just feeling a little trapped in there."

"Was he harassing you? Do we need to report him?"

"No, no. Of course not." She hesitated, then figured Linda would learn about it soon enough. "One of the inmates tried to grab me before court started."

Linda gasped. "Tried to or did?"

"Well, did. Sort of."

Fury sparkled in Linda's eyes. "And how'd he get that close to you? I can't believe Dom let that happen. What an idiot."

"It wasn't his fault. Another deputy was manning the in-custody room and the inmate got away from him. Dominic—I mean, Deputy Jeffries subdued him."

"I can tell that's not the end to the story, is it?"

She licked her lips, weighing honesty with the likelihood that Linda would tease her incessantly about Dominic's invitation. "Well, afterward he—he asked me out to dinner."

Linda laughed. "I told you I thought something was up. The guy can't keep his eyes off you. He just decided for some reason today that he was through trying to hide it. So does this mean you're canceling your date with Ty?"

"What? Of course not." Inside, she winced, because truthfully she'd forgotten all about the date. Mattie walked down the steps and headed for the parking lot across the street.

"You turned him down?"

"Great deduction, counselor."

"So you're not attracted to the buff bailiff in the least?"

Not in the least. The words were on the tip of the tongue, but so was a snide "Liar, liar, pants on fire." She opted for silence. Mattie was five feet from her car when she groaned. "I left my purse in the break room." Trying to get away from Dominic's probing gaze had zapped her memory.

"I'll go back with you." Linda linked her arm through Mattie's and began walking, forcing Mattie to either keep up with her much longer stride or be dragged along. Hoping to forestall any more questions about Dom, she asked, "What about the burglary? Do the police have any leads?"

Shaking her head, Linda said, "No. It's going to take a bit longer than eighteen hours for them to find anything." They walked in silence for a few seconds and Mattie had just started to relax when Linda said softly, "Someday, you're going to have to take a chance again, Mattie."

Mattie clenched her jaw. "Have you forgotten your friend? The one you set me up with? Doesn't that count?" They entered the main hallway and followed it to the judge's chambers.

"Of course, but I have a feeling you're not really interested in—"

Mattie opened the door and froze in shock.

Judge Butler—the respected Judge Butler; the married Judge Butler who had mentored Mattie for years—was on his knees in front of Brenda. She was perched on the table, naked from the waist down, legs spread, eyes closed in pleasure.

Mattie took a step back. "Ew." She wasn't sure if she'd spoken out loud or not. *I eat at that table,* she thought.

Brenda's eyes popped open and the judge slowly turned his head until his eyes met Mattie's. Mattie quickly shut the door and speed-walked away, Linda right beside her.

Linda clung to Mattie's arm. "Oh my gosh, did you see—"

"Of course I saw," Mattie hissed.

"Poor Mrs. Butler."

Poor us, Mattie thought. *Poor me.* She would probably carry the picture of Judge Butler and his court clerk to her grave.

"Or maybe I shouldn't be so quick to give Mrs. Butler my sympathy. He seemed pretty skilled at what he was doing. Granted, he was using his skill on another woman. Brenda didn't look too disappointed—"

"You're babbling, Linda."

"My eyes are still burning."

They barreled through the outer doors and froze. Mattie suddenly burst out laughing at the way Linda's thoughts echoed her own. She clamped a hand over her mouth, but her hysterical laughter burst through her fingers. She doubled over as Linda dragged her to the parking lot.

A minute later, Linda leaned against Mattie's car, gripping her aching side. "Do you think he saw us?"

"Brenda looked straight at me. Even if he didn't see us, she'll tell him." But she knew he'd seen them. Seen her. And he hadn't looked embarrassed either. He'd looked satisfied. Almost as if he'd wanted her to see him.

They looked at one another and burst out laughing again. "Do you think she calls him 'Your Honor' in bed?" Linda whispered.

Mattie groaned and slid down the side of the car until she was sitting on the ground, her skirt flared out next to her. "I can't believe I'm laughing about the fact that a man—Judge Butler, one of the county's most respected judges—is cheating on his wife." Her laughter had vanished and tears pricked her eyes. "What is wrong with people? Doesn't anyone keep their promises anymore?"

Linda just shrugged.

It might be different if Mattie didn't know Judge Butler's wife, but she was a kind, loving woman who adored her husband and had made brownies with Jordan. She was going to be devastated when she found out.

Mattie gasped as the ramifications of what she'd seen sank in. "Oh, God. What are we going to do?"

Linda reached out her hand to help Mattie to her feet. "We do nothing."

"But don't we have some kind of duty to report him? He's a public servant. Aren't there rules about judicial ethics?"

"Mattie, you're a single mother trying to make it on your own. I'm just starting to make headway on my career. What do you think reporting the judge's little indiscretion is going to do to either one of us? That's even assuming anyone believes us. No," she said, "We pretend like it never happened. We didn't see a thing."

"But there are two of us. You're a prosecutor. Why would you lie?"

"Why would a judge be stupid enough to get caught in such a compromising position? Look, let's just get out of here, okay? I don't want him following us and trying to explain, do you?"

"No. No, I don't want to hear anything he has to say about it."

Mattie moved to open her car door, then groaned. "My keys. They're still in my purse." She bit her lip. "Should we see if they've left?"

"No way. I'll drive you home and pick you up in the morning."

They looked at each other, their nervous amusement gone, the tense reality of what they'd witnessed bearing down on them. "Hey, Linda?"

"Yeah?"

"Lay off about Deputy Jeffries, okay?"

Linda glanced behind her, back at the building where a little bit more of their dwindling idealism had been left behind. She tightened her lips and nodded. "You bet. And I'll even do you one better. I'll do my best to keep him distracted and away from you."

The thought of Linda "distracting" Dom didn't sit well with Mattie, which was ridiculous, she told herself. All the more reason to have Linda do it. Still, even as Mattie smiled and nodded, she imagined how hurt she'd be if the distraction actually worked.

Chapter 8

"**D**amn him!" Two minutes after Linda dropped her off at home, her hands shaking, Mattie cursed Judge Butler for once again confirming that men couldn't be trusted. Hoping to calm down, she paced outside, then juggled her files in order to get to her cell, which she'd slipped back into her pocket rather than her purse. She dialed Ty Martinez's number. When he answered, she asked for a rain check, only saying that something unexpected had happened. She could tell by his voice he wasn't happy with her, but rather than feeling bad about that, she felt relieved.

She'd been distracted lately. Confused about her priorities. All a relationship would bring her was heartache and she'd had enough of that to last her a lifetime. Maybe when things settled down, she'd be more interested in getting to know Ty better. But right now...

She slipped her phone back in her pocket and was heading up the walk when her leg slipped on the path still damp from the automatic sprinklers. Whimpering, she caught herself on her palms, scraping them and her right knee, but not before she dropped her armful of files and the bag full of Judge Butler's offerings. Nose just inches from the sidewalk, she stared at the mottled concrete through a sheen of tears. "Damn him," she whispered, head hanging, knowing in her heart it wasn't so much Judge Butler that she cursed as it was Dominic.

She'd moved on. She'd been able to go days without thinking of him, and given the similarity between him and Jordan, that was saying something. Now he was back, not content to keep his distance but wanting…what?

Slowly, she straightened until she was sitting upright, knees pulled to her chest, forehead resting on her knees. Exhaustion wrapped around her and for a moment she was tempted to simply hide in the dimly lit shadows cast from the setting sun and the light on her front porch.

The muffled sound of footsteps had her scrambling to her feet. Across the street, a man slowly walked toward her, his head down, and his features covered by the bill of his baseball cap and his upturned coat collar.

Bending over, her hair covering half her face, Mattie quickly picked up the files she'd dropped. It was only when she straightened that she noticed the man had stopped moving and appeared to be staring at her. For a moment, she thought of Dom, but the man was too short and too thin to be him. Arms tightening around her files, she took a step closer, straining to see the man's features. "Can I help you?" she called.

He tilted his head slightly, indicating he'd heard her, but he didn't move. Didn't respond. The scrapes on her palms and knee throbbed, but couldn't compare to the sudden chill of fear that danced down the length of her spine. She took one step back. Then another. Then she was spinning around, running toward her front door, and pushing back one of the bushes where she always hung a spare key. She fumbled to open the screen door, looking over her shoulder to check whether the man was coming after her.

She couldn't see him. Automatically, she checked to the right, to the left, and then in front of her again.

But he was gone.

Her heart slammed against her chest. She forcibly stopped herself from shoving open the door. She couldn't go inside yet. Not until she was calm. She couldn't frighten Jordan or Tony. She wouldn't.

With watchful eyes and her hand still poised on the door handle, she took several deep breaths and tried to will her rattling heartbeat to slow. As she calmed, she began to feel foolish. She scolded herself for overreacting. It had probably been some kid trying to amuse himself. Or someone who'd thought the woman sitting on the sidewalk might be a little too kooky to talk to.

She shook her head. Dom's presence, his sudden come-on, and the judge's deplorable behavior were obviously making her more jumpy than normal. She pushed the door open and stepped inside her house, pasting an unconcerned expression on her face.

"Mommy!"

Mattie's anxiety seemed to drop away as soon as she got inside. Jordan barreled toward her and wrapped her arms around her. Dropping her files on the foyer console, Mattie buried her face in her little girl's neck and let the sweet smell of strawberry shampoo and dough wash over her. "I missed you, sweet girl," she murmured.

"I missed you, too." Jordan wriggled out of Mattie's arms and grabbed her hand, pulling her toward the kitchen "Come see what me and Uncle Tony made."

"Uncle Tony and I. And is it animal, vegetable or mineral?"

Jordan giggled. "None of the above."

"Well, I can't imagine what it is, then."

Jordan motioned her closer and whispered in her ear. "It's apple pie."

Mattie straightened, stuffing back her automatic pain at the combined echo of her and Dom's voices, both of them fantasizing about their perfect home together:

"...we'll pack up whatever we can carry in the back of my truck," he'd said. *"We'll drive during the day and camp out at night, making love in front of a fire. We'll stop at coffee shops to find the perfect apple pie and—"*

"—when we drive into a town with wide streets," she'd interrupted, *"and see a house for sale with a big wraparound porch and blue shutters, we'll know we can stop. You'll get a job at the local police department and I'll set up a little art studio, baking in my spare time until I call you home from work and surprise you with a hand-sewn baby quilt hanging over the front porch railing—yellow, because we won't find out the baby's sex until it's born."*

"Mommy?"

Jerking back and staring into a feminine version of Dominic's blue eyes, Mattie chastised herself. *Get it together. Jordan's been through enough.* "Wow, really? Apple pie is my favorite."

Jordan giggled. "I know."

She followed Jordan into the kitchen and pressed her lips together to keep from laughing.

Her brother Tony stood at the center island with a sappy look on his face. His brown hair, even curlier than hers, lent him a boyish quality that had been the bane of his existence, at least until he'd grown into his lanky limbs and filled out a little. When he'd been in college, he'd learned to work the hair along with a roguish smile. But then the drugs had started, and for six years, he'd fought the addiction off and on. In and out of rehab, he'd vacillated between the brother she knew and loved, and the sullen, distrustful brother she feared. His last stint in rehab, however, seemed to stick. He'd been off the drugs for over two years now, with no apparent relapses. He'd packed on muscle again, his cheeks no longer gaunt or his eyes shadowed. She was finally allowing herself to believe that her brother was back and here to stay; otherwise, she would never have let him care for Jordan, even for the two short hours that he had. It seemed her trust had been rewarded.

Tony was wearing one of her aprons, the one that said, Kiss the Cook, and he had flour on the tip of his nose. Nine-year-old Jordan, on the other hand, was spotless.

"You're just in time to help us put the pie in the oven."

Jordan ran off, shouting, "I just started *High School Musical*."

Mattie walked to her brother and kissed his cheek, so grateful that he was back in their lives. "How'd she wrangle you into this?"

"I had fun with her." His expression turned somber. "Thanks for trusting me, Mattie." Though he tried to hide it by looking away, Mattie saw the old shadow of guilt in his eyes.

"Don't be silly, Tony. I owe you." Wearily, Mattie walked to the sink, turned the water on, and winced when she placed her hands under the tap.

Tony immediately strode toward her. "What happened to your hands?"

She rolled her eyes. "You know me. Graceful as ever. I slipped on the walkway and skinned them. I'm fine." Grabbing a kitchen towel, she dried her hands, then fell into one of the kitchen chairs and propped her chin on her hand. She traced a water mark on the table with her finger.

"So what else is wrong, then?"

She glanced up. "A defendant got a little unruly today—"

Tony covered his eyes with his hands and groaned. "I knew it. I can always tell when you're hiding something." He lowered his hands and propped his hands on his hips. "Are you okay? What happened?"

"I'm fine. He barely grabbed my arm before the bailiff cuffed him. I'm more upset that the bailiff got it into his head to ask me out."

"Smart guy," Tony offered loyally.

She smiled. "Thanks, little brother." She hesitated, then decided not to tell Tony the bailiff was the same man who'd broken her heart in college.

Tony walked over and grabbed her hands, releasing them immediately when she winced. "Sorry, sorry." He pulled her into a hug, released her, then retrieved a tube from the first-aid kit she kept under the sink. Coming closer, he removed the top from the tube of Neosporin.

"I can—"

He pulled the tube away from her reach and glared at her.

With a sigh, she held out her hands and he smeared them with the thick gel. The sting in her hands increased, then subsided to a dull throb. Tony blew on her palms, just as she would have done for Jordan. Finally satisfied, he put the medicine back where he'd found it, then washed his hands. "You didn't park in the garage. Did someone drive you home?"

"Uh, yeah, I got a lift."

Tony threw the kitchen towel down and crossed his arms over his chest. "Linda?"

Mattie grimaced. "Yeah. Linda." She couldn't lie, but suddenly she wished she'd taken a cab instead of letting Linda drive her home. Although she and Tony had dated for six months, they'd broken up over two years ago, towards the beginning of Tony's last relapse, and she knew there wasn't a day that went by that Tony didn't regret it.

Tony stepped back, turned and loaded the unbaked pie into the oven. "So, is she dating?"

"No. I don't know. She hasn't mentioned anyone."

"That doesn't mean—"

A low buzzing cut Tony off. He reached into his pocket and pulled out his cell phone. He frowned as he looked at the screen. "Just a sec, Mattie." Bringing the phone to his ear, he turned his body away from her. "This is Tony." He glanced at her over his shoulder. "No. I'm not interested. I already told you that." He listened for several minutes, his lips pressed into a grim line. "I can't talk now. Let me call you back." He flipped his phone shut and returned it to his pocket before running a hand through his hair. "I should be going."

"You don't want to stay and have some pie with us?"

"No, you'll have to tell me what you think. Eat at your own risk. I've got plans tonight."

She tried to sound casual when she asked, "Who with?"

Tony's face tightened in anger. "Don't, Mattie. Please. I don't need you or anyone else keeping tabs on me, okay?"

Mattie nodded, automatically biting back her annoyance. "Fine." Then she remembered. "Hang on a second. Judge Butler gave me something for you. Let me go get it."

"Judge Butler? Why would he—?"

But Mattie was already striding toward the foyer where she'd put down the bag. She found the envelope that had Tony's name on it and brought it over to him. "He asked how you were." She tilted her head, puzzled by the way Tony stared at the envelope as if it was going to bite him. "What's wrong?"

"Huh?" Tony looked up, grabbed the envelope from her and stuffed it in his back pocket. "Nothing. It's probably a gift certificate for a round of golf at his country club. He's been nagging me to go back."

Confusion marred her brow. "Back? When did you go the first time?"

"I'm going, short stuff," Tony called out.

"Bye, Uncle Tony!" Jordan yelled back.

Tony headed for the kitchen door and opened it.

"Tony, wait!" Mattie rushed up to him and lightly grasped his arms. "I forgot to tell you, I'm not going to leave a spare key outside the house anymore. I—I just think with Jordan, it would be better…" She paused lamely and before she could continue, Tony nodded.

"Good idea. A lot of unsavory elements out there. Can't be too safe."

Knowing what he was thinking, she almost winced. "We're okay, right?"

Her brother smiled and she could see the regret in his eyes that she even had to ask. "We're fine, Mattie. You have enough to worry about, so don't worry about me. I know you had to at one time, but that's over." He stepped outside, then grinned at her over his shoulder. "Hey, maybe this bailiff guy can deliver on some fun. You deserve to have fun, Mattie."

Mattie shrugged. "Right now, my idea of fun is a nice, boring night at home watching a movie with Jordan. So I've got everything I need."

Tony shook his head and sighed. "I know, babe. That's what bothers me more than anything." Tony leaned in, kissed her cheek and said, "See you later."

She locked the door behind him and pushed aside the curtains that covered the glass pane to watch him get into his truck. He waved at her and called out, "Bye, mother," which she heard clearly even through the door. She laughed and turned away, hugging her arms to her chest.

She sank back into her chair and laid her head on her arms. For a brief moment, she thought about Judge Butler, and what she and Linda had walked in on. Then she thought of Dom and the look in his eyes as he'd caressed her arm.

Both incidents had been disturbing. Still, she enjoyed the shiver of heat her thoughts of Dom generated, even as she swore to stop fantasizing about the man once and for all.

Chapter 9

Thursday

The next morning, as everyone in the courtroom waited for the judge to return after a short break, Dom knew something was up. Mattie seemed even more tense around him, and not just because he'd asked her to dinner. She seemed to avoid everyone. She avoided even looking at anyone. Anyone except her friend, Linda.

On the other hand, the D.A., who'd seemed more keen on taunting Dom than seducing him, was now hitting on him harder than an anvil on steel. It didn't escape his notice, however, that she only did it when both he and Mattie were around. She obviously wanted him to stay away from her friend and wasn't above using her impressive cleavage and long legs to make that happen.

Her sudden turnaround filled him with conflict.

On the one hand, it pissed him off. Normally, Mattie wasn't

a coward and their past didn't excuse her playing petty games with him and her friend. On the other hand, the fact that she'd resorted to such measures must mean that he'd gotten to her and she was running scared. And not because she wasn't interested. He trusted his instincts when it came to women and she was still interested, just wary. That wasn't exactly a relief. Given the explosive chemistry between them, he wasn't sure they could fight it off for much longer. Maybe he could resist his own feelings, but knowing Mattie wanted him? Could he really walk away from that temptation again? He couldn't even tell himself that staying away from her was what the job required. Given Dusty's attack and the package that Judge Butler had asked Mattie to deliver to her brother, he should be getting closer to her. It was the reason he'd asked her to dinner, or at least that's what he told himself. After all, Brenda had strongly hinted Mattie was single and Mattie had pretty much confirmed it when he'd asked whether her *boyfriend* could pick up her daughter. So whatever it took to get the job done, right?

It didn't hurt that every time he thought of her single status, his heart rate picked up and a sense of possessive satisfaction filled him. He wanted to get close to her again, figure out the intricacies of the woman she'd become and, if it helped him do his job, all the better, right? Only he hated the thought of using her that way, even if it would be to help find Joel's killer.

Because the only other person he'd loved more than Joel was Mattie.

Realization shuddered through him. Mattie was single. Yes, he had a job to do. Yes, getting close to her could help with that. But those were the things that had brought him to her, not reasons to stay away from her. Unlike with Joel, he had a second shot here. For what, he wasn't sure, but he wasn't going to give up the chance to find out.

"Excuse me, Linda," he said, interrupting the woman's flirting act. "I need to talk to Mattie."

"Oh but—"

As he headed towards Mattie, her eyes widened. He cocked a brow and smiled, but his smile vanished when a tall, dark-haired man in an expensive suit laid his palms over Mattie's eyes from behind like a blindfold.

Mattie jumped, turned and smiled.

Dom stopped in his tracks.

As they spoke, Mattie repeatedly touched her hair. At one point, she even flipped it over her shoulder. When the man caressed her cheek with the back of his knuckles, a low, angry sound rumbled from Dom's throat. Automatically, he took a step forward.

But someone caught his arm.

It was Linda. "You might not want to do that, Deputy."

He glanced swiftly towards Mattie. The suit had left and, although he caught Mattie's eye, she turned quickly away. Slowly, he turned back to Linda. "Something I can do for you?"

She pursed her lips. "Nice try, but I don't buy it. Just what's going on with you and Mattie?"

"How about you answer that question for me?"

Her expression tightened before she glanced over his shoulder. "Court's about to start."

As she walked away, Dom took his place next to the bench. Brenda announced the judge's arrival.

If he hadn't been watching Mattie so closely, he might have missed it. When the judge walked in, she immediately tensed and averted her eyes. Then she glanced back at Linda, whose eyes had widened. Linda shook her head frantically, her urgency unmistakable.

Dom frowned. Yes, something was definitely up with these two. He was going to find out what.

* * *

Mattie breathed a sigh of relief as soon as Judge Butler declared court over for the day. The air in the courtroom had thickened with each passing minute, refusing to fill her lungs. She felt oddly dizzy, certain that for the past two hours, Judge Butler, Dominic, Linda and Brenda had taken turns staring at her. She couldn't even tell herself that Dominic's attention was sexual. His normally placid expression had shifted into a permanent frown.

She and Linda obviously sucked at subterfuge. However, the more time she'd spent in court, the more certain she'd become that she couldn't just ignore what she'd seen yesterday. But what on earth could she do? Feeling overwhelmed and bitter, she rushed to pack up her stenograph. She jumped when Judge Butler called to her.

Nervously, she licked her lips. She stared at his chin, trying not to remember where it and the rest of his face had been yesterday. "Yes, your honor?"

"You seem distracted. Everything okay?"

Swallowing hard, she raised her gaze to his. There was no guilt. No embarrassment. "I'm fine. A little tired, that's all. It's been a difficult case."

Understanding lit his eyes. "Yes, I imagine with Jordan at home, it would be especially difficult hearing about the abuse the victim in this case suffered. Your work is always appreciated though. By the way, did you give Tony my letter?"

"Yes. He said thank you." When Judge Butler nodded and turned away, she couldn't stop herself from asking, "How's Mrs. Butler, by the way?"

Brenda, who'd moved to follow the judge, glared at her. Judge Butler merely smiled. "She's fine, thank you." He turned to Brenda. "Do you have the evidence log from today?"

Turning to face Mattie, Brenda didn't even bother to look

guilty. Instead, she murmured, "Yes, Your Honor. I have everything you need."

When the pair of them disappeared, Mattie turned to leave. The sooner she got away from this place the better. She gasped when she brushed against Dominic. The man was making a habit of sneaking up on her.

She edged away from him, but still managed to brush her arm against his again. Although the light material of her suit jacket blocked contact with the firm muscle of his forearm, she swore his warmth penetrated the fabric. Breathing deep, she struggled not to close her eyes at the clean, masculine smell of him.

She stared at the strong column of his throat, wondering whether he would still taste the same if she licked him. "Yes?"

"Linda can't make dinner. She said to tell you that an emergency came up and that I should walk you to your car."

She glared at him. "Now, why would she do that? Considering that I'm quite capable of taking care of myself."

"Court was still in session. She got a phone call and had to leave." He crossed his arms over his chest and peered down at her indulgently as if she were a recalcitrant child. "Looks like you didn't tell her about me, huh? Or did you? Was that what the hot and heavy come-ons were about? Some kind of weird competition thing?"

Mattie tried to feign innocence. "I don't know what you're talking about."

He didn't look convinced. "She asked me to escort you to your car, and I promised I would. You don't want me to break a promise, do you?"

She bit her lip to stop her automatic retort. Raising her hand, she tucked back her hair, then silently groaned when his eyes narrowed. He gently took hold of both her wrists. Automatically, she closed her fingers into fists, but winced when the movement irritated her already sore skin.

Frowning, he rubbed his thumbs against her closed fingers as if to urge them open. "What happened?"

"I fell."

"That's it?"

"That's it." She pulled her hands away and he reluctantly released her.

"Why don't you tell me what's going on with the judge?"

Unable to stop herself, Mattie took a step back. Had Linda said something to him? "What are you talking about?"

"It was obvious you and the D.A. reacted strongly when he came in. Did you catch him getting down and dirty with Brenda?"

Horrified, her cheeks burning, she stared at him. "You know?"

He shrugged. "Of course."

Mattie scowled. "What, do you guys go out for drinks and brag about your conquests?"

Instantly, she wanted to recall the words, especially when he just stared at her with mild reproof.

"Did the judge see you?"

Biting her lip, she looked around. The courtroom had cleared. "I think so."

"What was he doing?"

"What?"

"What. Was. He. Doing."

She flushed even hotter.

He grinned. "Ah. That good, huh?"

"Yes. I mean, no," she hissed. "Not good. Not good at all. I don't ever want to eat on the break room table again."

"Was he giving or receiving?"

He didn't need to expand on his question. Vivid images flashed in her head, none of them of Judge Butler and Brenda, all of them of her and Dom. He'd been a generous lover, one who hadn't been afraid to push her despite her inexperience. "Why on earth does that matter?" she managed to choke out.

He pressed his lips together in a failed attempt to hide his amusement. "Because if he was giving, he probably didn't have a good enough view to see anything."

"Ha, ha," she muttered. "I never realized you were so funny." She moved fast, slipping past him and through the courtroom doors.

Undeterred, he followed her. "You don't realize a lot of things about me."

"Such as?"

"Such as, when I want something, I do whatever it takes to get it."

That made her stumble slightly, but she compensated by picking up speed. When they reached the outer door that would lead them to the courthouse steps, he pushed it open for her. She breezed past him, marched down the steps, then gasped when he grabbed her arm and pulled her body into his. They were chest to chest, his hard thighs pressing against her. She looked up at him, willing herself to remember his rejection. "Actually, I did realize that, Dominic. You showed me exactly how much you wanted, or rather didn't want me, ten years ago. You want something from me now, but this time you're not going to get it."

"Why is that? It's what you want, too."

She nearly choked. "You're arrogant."

"I meant you want to clear the air just as much as I do," he clarified. He released her and she stepped back. Flexing a brow, he asked, "What did you think I meant?"

"Oh, I don't know," she said sweetly. "But by the way your body was pressed up against mine, I have a pretty good guess."

Instead of being embarrassed, he looked down and studied his erection, clearly straining against the fly of his pants.

"What can I say? Being attracted to you has never been a problem for me."

"Thankfully, I can't say the same."

Amazement flashed across his face before he stepped closer, their bodies almost brushing again. Her chest heaved with the effort it took to keep breathing, and he glanced at her breasts before capturing her gaze. Softly, he urged, "Don't mistake me for other men you know. I'm not a cheat and I'm not a wimp. I'm honest. I always have been. Our attraction to one another was hot enough that I can still feel the heat. You couldn't handle me becoming a cop and I wasn't going to be the cause of a lifetime of resentment. But your body still wants mine as much as I want yours."

"You're imagining things," she breathed.

"Am I?"

"I'm not getting involved with you again, Dom. It hurt too much the first time."

He cursed. "Damn it, Mattie. That was ten years ago. We both made mistakes."

"Yes. Mistakes I don't plan to repeat." She pulled away. "Goodbye, Deputy Jeffries." She paused to open her purse and take out her car keys. She fished around for a few seconds, then stopped short to stare at the contents of her bag.

Things were out of order. Mattie always kept her red Liz Claiborne wallet in the front inner pocket, but it was in the main compartment of the bag. In addition, her brush was gone. Her money, however, hadn't been touched.

"What's wrong?"

Her head jerked up and she shook it to clear it. Was she imagining things? But no, her brush was gone and she hadn't been the one to take it out.

Dominic peered over her shoulder and into the contents of her purse. "Is something missing?"

"Just my brush. But it looks like my wallet's been moved."

"You're sure?"

"Well, no. I can't be sure. I'm pretty predictable though." She waved her hand in a dismissive gesture. "Maybe I'm just imagining things." But then she remembered the man outside her house. Had she been imagining things then, too? Unease rose within her, making her frown.

"You leave your keys in your purse? Inside the break room?"

"Yes."

"Locked up?"

"We don't have lockers. Just a cabinet where we all keep our things. Why?"

"If you think your purse was tampered with, you might want to get your locks changed. It would have been easy for someone to take your keys and put them back this morning."

Again, she thought of the man she'd seen across the street from her house last night and fear made her tremble. He obviously noticed.

"Damn it, I'm not trying to scare you, Mattie. I just want you to be careful."

Her eyes widened at the vehemence in his voice. When she spoke, her voice expressed every bit of the confusion she felt. "Why are you here? What do you want from me, Dom?"

"Right now?" His jaw clenched. "How about we start with your forgiveness? I know I hurt you ten years ago, Mattie. Believe me when I say I hurt myself just as much, if not more."

It was all suddenly too much for her. Her anxiety about Jordan, her ridiculous feeling of betrayal at Judge Butler's actions, her concern for Tony and her unexpected reunion with Dom. Her eyes stung and she blinked quickly, desperately trying to hold back her tears. "I—I don't know if I can give you what you're asking for, Dom." She closed her eyes, took a deep breath, and shook her head, feeling like a fool.

She gasped when he hooked a finger under her chin and

gently nudged until she looked at him. "I can accept that. For now. But how about dinner? Can you give me that much, at least?"

"I don't know—" she began, but he talked over her.

"I've wanted to try the Mexican place nearby. You had plans with Linda, so your daughter's with someone else, isn't she?"

"Yes, she's spending the night at a friend's. But—" Biting her lip, she hesitated. She suddenly felt as if the answer to his question was going to have a huge effect on her life. *It's just dinner,* she reasoned. She wasn't going to date him. Or marry him. Or sleep with him.

Was she?

The heated look in his eyes indicated he knew the treacherous path her thoughts had taken. Obviously encouraged, his hand slipped under her hair to cup her neck and slowly massage the back of her scalp. She bit her lip to keep from moaning.

He wanted to kiss her. She could see it in his eyes and knew her yearning was reflected in her own eyes as well. "I—I—" She stopped, not knowing what to say, just knowing it should be "no."

"I love the wetness factor, you know."

She swallowed hard. "Wetness?" she squeaked.

The desire in his eyes flared into something so hot, so intense, that it should have incinerated her. Instead, it made her gravitate even closer to him.

"Definitely," he murmured, leaning down until his breath ruffled the hair next to her ear. His thumb pressed into some secret spot that only he'd ever found, and she couldn't stop the soft, breathless moan that escaped her.

"That's right. You know you want it, baby."

His words jolted her. Seemed so out of character that she pulled back to see his face.

Confusion made her brows furrow.

Along with the heat was now amusement. A small smile tipped his lips.

"You do, don't you? Mild, medium, hot. Red sauce. Green sauce. But my favorite is mole. Have you ever had mole sauce, Mattie?"

"Mole?" Eyes narrowing, she shoved him away. He laughed outright, and her annoyance was tempered by the sight of him expressing such joyful exuberance even if was at her expense.

She didn't let him know that, though.

"Why don't you take your mole sauce and—" she began.

"Oh, come on. You should have seen the look on your face. Besides, we both know if I told you what I really want, you'd be running for your car before the words were out of my mouth." He sobered, his eyes dropping to sweep her body before landing unerringly on *her* mouth. Raising his hand once more, he caressed her jaw. "I don't have to tell you what I want, Mattie. Because you know what it is. And you want the same thing."

The throbbing heat of desire was back so fast it made her dizzy.

They'd had their chance, she reminded herself. And it had ended in disaster.

Yet, she was reluctant to let their fragile reconnection end.

What would it hurt, she thought, for them to talk? Dinner wouldn't change things. She still had no intention of telling him about Jordan. Maybe she never would. But she could at least give him the chance to change her mind, right? So while she didn't say yes, exactly, she said the next best thing. "I've never tried mole. But maybe…maybe it's time I did."

As Dom escorted Mattie to the little Mexican restaurant three blocks from the courthouse he wondered if he shouldn't just make an excuse and veer her back toward her car instead. That little interchange they'd just had had almost knocked him off his feet. He'd seen the same struggle on her face that he'd been having—the temptation to take something you desperately wanted tempered by the knowledge that you couldn't possibly have it—and he'd wanted to howl in frustration.

In ten years, things had only gotten more complicated for them. There was still his job to consider—a job far more dangerous than the average cop's—but she also had a daughter now. And he couldn't forget he was here under false pretenses or that she was a potential target of Guapo's, if not more. Plus, she obviously had a personal relationship with Judge Butler, which could only make things more complicated. After all, he hadn't forgotten Joel's implication that Judge Butler might not be on the up and up.

None of that, however, lessened the sizzling attraction that sparked to life whenever they were together.

She still wanted him and all he could think about was her naked and under him, pulling him into the cradle she'd make of her arms and breasts and thighs. He'd enter her and pleasure them both and then he'd stay with her. He wouldn't get up and leave minutes after the deed was done, as he normally did with women these days. He'd hold her and caress her and play with her in a way he'd never allowed himself to play with a woman since their time together in college.

The yearning to have all that struck him so completely that he immediately flinched away from it. This wasn't about some sick need he had for respite, but about Joel. About finding his killer and insuring that Judge Butler and his staff weren't involved or in danger themselves.

He'd tried to be funny, but her response had only confirmed what he'd already known. Playing with Mattie could get addictive.

As they sat down, he tried to steer things back on track. "Was it a special occasion yesterday?"

She raised a brow. "Excuse me?"

"The judge got you a present, right?" And one for her brother.

She bristled. "If this is about the judge and me—"

"Has that been a problem for you in the past? People thinking you and Judge Butler—"

She shook her head and stood. "I should have known your offer wasn't about dinner or wanting to be with me. You want fodder for the rumor mill, is that it? Well, forget it. You and every other jerk out there who wants to make insinuations about Judge Butler and me can just—"

"Mattie." He put his hand on hers, sighing when she pulled it away. "Please don't go. Obviously I know the judge has no problem with acting certain ways off hours. I don't believe that about you and I never said I did. I was just curious, that's all. Trying to find out more about you. I'm sorry my attempt was so clumsy."

She sat down. "I don't want to talk about work. Especially Judge Butler."

"Okay. Tell me about you. For instance, I saw you talking to that suit in court today." The memory made renewed jealousy fill his veins. "You dating?"

Her brows lifted in surprise before she glanced away. "He's—interested."

"And what about you? Are you interested in him?"

Her gaze whipped back to his. "Why wouldn't I be? He's handsome. Sweet. I'm open to something developing."

Ah. The relief almost made him dizzy. He hadn't realized, however, that he'd smiled until she snapped, "What are you smiling for?"

"Sorry. It's what you didn't say that I'm smiling about." He leaned forward until his nose was just inches from her.

"You didn't say you were interested, Mattie. And if you were, you'd be more than 'open' to something developing, wouldn't you?"

"You're wrong."

No, he wasn't, he thought, but all he said was a mild, "Okay."

She looked suspicious for a minute, then said, "How about you? Are you seeing anyone special?"

"No."

"Well, that was a quick answer. Quick and firm."

He shrugged. "My career keeps me busy. Besides, after you, I guess I never found another woman who even remotely made me think of settling down."

She took a deep breath, looking stunned by his statement. When she couldn't seem to come up with a response, he took pity on her and changed the subject. "You wanted to be an artist when we were together, Mattie. What happened to that dream?"

She hesitated, then settled back into her seat. "I still paint. I just grew up and realized that to support myself, I needed to do something more practical."

"I guess it would be hard to be an artist with a daughter to raise." It was subtle, but he saw the way her eyes immediately shuttered. "What, you don't want to talk about your daughter, either? Why?"

The angle of her chin became mutinous. "Why do you?"

"This isn't a police station or a courtroom, Mattie. I'm not interrogating or cross-examining you. Who knows, if this evening goes well and we can put the past behind us, maybe I can even meet her sometime."

"That's never going to happen," she said.

He stared at her, hurt despite himself. "Which part? Putting the past behind us or meeting your daughter?"

She said nothing for several tense moments, then forced

a smile. "Look, Dominic. We had two months together ten years ago. You're practically a stranger to me now. But despite how I've been acting, there's no reason we can't be civil to each other for the rest of the month. You've done your part to try to mend things between us and I can do the same."

Reaching out, she covered his hand with hers. "Okay?"

He immediately curled his fingers around hers. The sight of their joined hands made his chest hurt. So did her comment about them being strangers. It made him want to pull her against him and remind her just how intimately acquainted they were and could be again. Instead, he squeezed her fingers once more, then let go to sit back. "You're right, but as coworkers we shouldn't be strangers either. So ask me something. Get to know me again."

"Anything?" She looked dubious and he didn't blame her in the least. "And you'll answer? Truthfully?"

"I'll answer unless there's a job-related reason why I can't. How's that?"

"Not much of a guarantee, that's for sure." She seemed to ponder his words before shrugging. "What the heck. It'll be nice to be the one asking questions for once. How long have you been rock climbing?"

Surprised at her choice of question, he said, "About eight years." He held up a hand and grinned sheepishly. "And yes, before you ask, I deliberately followed you to the gym that day. Seeing you again blew me away and I just didn't want to let you go yet. I'm sorry if I made you uncomfortable."

She arched her brows but let his comment pass without responding. "Do you ever climb real mountains without a safety line?"

He hesitated for a second but eventually opted for the truth. "I have a few times, but lots of people do it. It's called bouldering, Mattie. And I've worked my way up to it. I wouldn't do it if I truly thought I'd be at risk."

"Right." She studied him for a minute before continuing. "So what about this job? Why are you here temporarily? Why at all? Somehow, I think your talents are being wasted here."

Relieved that they'd somehow gotten past the last disastrous minutes, he thought about her question. He hadn't made any headway on Joel's murder. Hadn't found anything implicating Judge Butler, his staff, or Guapo. But he couldn't say any of that to Mattie. Instead, he simply said, "It's a standard rotation for all sheriff's deputies. Like I told you before, I go where I'm needed."

"Until something better comes along?"

He sighed even though there'd been no edge to her words, only curiosity. "Until my usefulness is tapped out," he corrected. "Sometimes it's not about moving on to better things, but about no longer being needed. Or about doing more harm than good if I stay."

He hoped Mattie heard what he was really trying to say. That he'd left her to insure her own happiness as much as his. But if she understood, she didn't say anything.

She took another sip of water. Then, with a small, teasing smile on her lips, leaned toward him. "There's something else I've been dying to ask you, Dom," she murmured.

His muscles tightened and his gaze dropped to her lips, slick and shiny with the water she'd drunk. "What's that, Mattie-mine?"

"What the heck is mole sauce actually made with?"

Dinner passed quickly and enjoyably.

Mattie discovered mole tasted better than she would have expected based on Dominic's description. Even more surprising, the more time they spent together, the closer she got to indeed forgiving him. And herself. They *had* been young. As he'd said, they'd both made mistakes.

He paid the bill—getting a dangerous look in his eyes

when she tried to pay her share—and walked her back to the parking garage, his hand resting comfortably at the small of her back. To her dismay, she found herself walking slower to enjoy his company a while longer.

Words piled up in her throat. She wanted to tell him more about her life. To brag about Jordan. To unload her fears about her and Tony. To tell him she'd been wrong in trying to pressure him to give up his dreams.

Instead, what she said was, "My husband was a cop."

He stopped on the sidewalk, obviously as surprised by her comment as she was.

Feeling foolish, she twisted her hands together and focused on a point just over his shoulder. "After you left, I was so angry. At you, but also myself." She swallowed and faced him. Faced her own part in their breakup. "I drove you away with my stupid fears."

"They weren't stupid, Mattie—"

She shook her head. "Don't. Please. I need to say this."

After a second, he nodded, encouraging her to continue.

"I started hanging out at cop bars. I don't know, I guess I thought if I met someone who was already a cop, I'd—I'd be that much closer to having a part of you, too. And then I met John and I thought, don't mess this up again. Maybe he's your second chance."

The muscles in his jaw ticked before he asked, "What happened?"

She smiled sadly. "John wasn't just a cop, he was an adrenaline junkie. He bought a motorcycle, and kept upgrading to the newest and fastest thing. Even though we couldn't afford it. Even though I kept telling him it was too dangerous—"

"You ended up being right, didn't you?"

"He wrapped his motorcycle around a pole a few months before our sixth anniversary. It wasn't because of the job. He was off-duty at the time, fooling around with some friends.

So I learned my lesson, Dom. It's not a person's job that gets in the way of our choices, it's what a person's willing to do and not do. I just didn't know how to say it back then."

Reaching out, he took both her hands in his. "I'm sorry."

She stared at their joined hands before slipping hers away. "So am I. He was a wonderful person. But it was a long time ago. Almost another lifetime."

"You never married again?"

"I had Tony to help me with Jordan. Friends..."

"But a husband. A partner—"

She shook her head. "I couldn't go through it again."

"The heartache of losing a partner?"

"No, the heartache of losing a partner I was too boring to satisfy on my own."

He stared at her. "Is that what you really think?"

"It's what I know. You were the first one to teach me that lesson, Dom. My pressuring you to give up your dream only made it easier for you to leave me, but it would have happened eventually."

Eyes narrowing, he stared at her, his eyes focusing on the spot that joined her neck and shoulder. It made her insides explode with heat. She'd loved it when he'd kissed her there. More times than not, she'd go wild from that touch alone, acting in ways no one would dare say was boring.

"Come here, Mattie."

Her eyes widened in alarm. "Wh-why?"

He stepped closer, making a low sound in his throat—something that almost sounded like a growl—when she stepped back. "Because I want to show you just how boring you can be."

She gasped. The way he was looking at her, with pure sexual drive flaring in his eyes, made her achy and wet between her thighs. The temptation to walk into his arms and let passion take them was almost unbearable. She bit her lip and dug her nails into her palms, hoping the pain could somehow pull her back from the very dangerous edge she was balanced on.

For all her complaints about him, some people might say that Mattie had too easily replaced him. After all, only a few months had passed before she'd started dating John. Not long after, they'd married. Of course, she'd been pregnant and scared, and John had been kind. Did that make her weak? Was it so bad to want a man to build a life with?

When she was young, Mattie had naturally gravitated towards being in a relationship. She liked being part of a couple. Going on dates and holding hands. Having a man pick up the bill and hold the door open for her. The slight teasing banter when you knew the night was going to end in close, physical contact with someone you loved. She'd missed that in the past few years. Missed sex. Missed being held and having a man inside her.

Apparently, if she asked for that right now, Dom would give it to her. But he still couldn't give her what she really wanted. What she really needed. Because whether he admitted it or not, he was an adrenaline junkie, too. If she gave herself to him physically, he'd take her heart, as well. And she'd have to risk losing the only man she'd ever truly loved a second time. That thought enabled her to break free from the spell he'd cast. Shaking her head, she stepped back. "I can't do this," she said.

"Of course you can," he countered, looking undeterred. He stepped closer, and she held her palms out pleadingly.

"Let's say I did. Then what?"

As she'd known it would, the question froze him in his tracks. "Why do we have to answer that question?"

"Because I have a daughter to take care of," she reminded him. "And quite frankly, I've already been burned by you. You can't give me what I need."

His face tightened and she released her breath, thinking she'd finally made him see reason. Instead, he moved closer, placed his hands on her shoulders, kneading them softly. "I think I can give you exactly what you need. And what you want."

She whimpered at his words, unable to deny their veracity. Of their own volition, she lifted her arms and placed them around his neck. "We can't," she whispered, still trying to be logical even if her body wouldn't.

He slowly lowered his head, until all she could focus on were his blue eyes, blazing at her with masculine intent, and his hands, showing her what she could have.

Strong but gentle.

Hungry but generous.

She tilted her face up. Just the tiniest bit. *Yes,* she thought, as his lips met hers.

The first contact undid her. Doubt and resolve gave way to a blessed forgetfulness and left her solely a victim to sensation. Again, she thought in contrasts. His lips were so much softer than she remembered, but the way he opened them and angled his head for better positioning made her shiver. The way he used his tongue made her moan.

He'd always been an accomplished lover, but she could tell he'd gained even more experience. Before, he'd been controlled by a young man's passion. Now, he knew better than to invade when teasing would work so much better. His tongue dipped, then withdrew, tracing the bow of her lip before he nipped at the bottom.

"You taste the same," he whispered against them, not bothering to lift his head. "So damn sexy," he growled. "Like honey and cream, melting on my tongue."

She raised her hands to his face, cupping the hard planes of his jaw. Even that simple touch seemed to inflame him. Suddenly, his kiss wasn't so teasing anymore. His mouth widened. His hands lowered to her hips, pulling her body into his and she sighed with relief as her aching breasts rubbed up against him.

Wrenching his lips from hers, he buried his face in her neck, struggling to catch his breath. She tangled her fingers in his hair and unthinkingly soothed him, even as her own heartbeat threatened to pound out of her.

He lifted his head. "I want to do that again."

His blatant honesty compelled her to give the same. "I—I do too. But—" Her words were interrupted by the sound of breaking glass.

Mattie jerked and Dom's arms dropped away. From the direction of the parking garage, a horn began to honk repetitively. "Car alarm," he muttered. "Yours?"

She shook her head. She had a beat-up old Toyota that she couldn't get someone to steal even if she wanted him to.

Instinctively, she stepped forward but Dom put his arm in front of her. He activated the radio on his shoulder. "This is Deputy Jeffries. There's a disturbance in the south parking garage. Send someone out."

"Nichols will be out in three," replied the voice on the other end.

"You're not going to go in?"

Dominic looked sideways at Mattie. "I would, but then I'd be neglecting you. I'm just not that kind of guy."

"I thought that's just the kind of guy you were." She tried to sound teasing, but with her senses still sizzling from his kiss and her own desperate response, she sounded more accusatory than anything else. What had she been thinking? The instant the glass had broken and she'd seen that hard look come into his eyes—the cop look—it had snapped her back to reality, clearly reminding her why she needed to stay away from men in general. This man in particular.

His gaze sharpened. "Meaning?"

"Never mind—"

"What kind of man am I, Mattie?"

Feeling penned in, she raised her chin. "You and John had one thing in common, Dom, and it wasn't just being a cop. It's your need for adrenaline. You'll always take risks—"

"That's not true—"

"You climb walls without a harness. And you got pumped restraining that inmate Dusty. Admit it."

Before responding, he waved to a uniformed man who walked out of the courthouse and into the parking garage. Then he brought all his attention back to her, his eyes blazing. "I'm not admitting anything. I told you, I only take calculated risks and I don't climb without some kind of safety measure in place. As for Dusty, he deserved far worse than what he got for touching you."

Yowza. She had to admit the he-man protector bit he had going made her insides melt, but of course she couldn't let him know that.

Before she could respond, a voice on his radio interrupted them. "This is Deputy Nichols. I need an ambulance, stat."

Dominic engaged his radio. "What do you have?"

"I've got an unconscious woman here. She's been beaten bad."

"Did you find ID?"

"Government issued. She works here. In the D.A.'s office."

Mattie gasped, panic going off inside her like fireworks. Dominic placed his hand on her shoulder and spoke into his radio again. "What's her name?"

"Linda Delaney."

"Linda!" Cupping her hand over her mouth, Mattie lunged forward, her only thought that she needed to get to her friend. A heavy arm clamped around her waist and she screamed in frustration, trying to pull away.

Dominic lowered his head closer to hers. "Shh. Mattie,

stop. Listen to me. Someone's with her, and an ambulance is on the way."

Whimpering, Mattie shook her head. "I need to go to her. Let. Me. Go!"

"Mattie!" Dominic shook her gently, then cupped her face in his hands. "Look at me, Mattie. Look at me."

She stopped struggling and stared into his eyes. Her panicked breaths heaved in and out of her, and she couldn't hear past the pounding of her heart. His eyes, though—his blue, blue eyes. They grounded her. Gave her something to focus on so that the soft caress of his hands on her face finally registered. "The area isn't secure. The ambulance will be here soon and we'll get Linda to a hospital. But I need you to go inside."

"Ambulance," she breathed.

He nodded and straightened. "Yes. Now, let me get you inside. I'll go to her immediately and find out her condition, I promise. But first I need to make sure you're okay. I have to keep my promise to Linda and keep you safe. Okay?"

"Yes. Okay." Tears burned her lids and she grasped at the front of Dominic's shirt. "Please check on her and tell me she's okay. Please."

"I'll check on her. Find out if anyone noticed anything or anyone suspicious."

"Like what?" Even to herself, she sounded like she was barely holding it together. But Linda— "This place is always crawling with thugs."

His jaw clenched. "Some thugs are more memorable than others. Now come on, let's get you inside."

Chapter 10

Mattie paced in the hallway just inside the courthouse's lower level glass doors. It had been five minutes since Dominic had disappeared to check on Linda. An ambulance as well as several police cars were now parked on the street in front of the parking garage. Every once in a while, someone in a blue or tan uniform would move into her view, but not one of them was Dominic. "Where are they?" she moaned, referring not just to Dominic, but the two paramedics she'd seen jump out of the back of the ambulance with a gurney. "Why hasn't he checked in with you?"

Marcus O'Neil, the young deputy whom Dominic had assigned to stay with her, placed a comforting hand on her shoulder. "They're going to want to check your friend over before they move her. It hasn't been that long, honest."

Biting her lip, Mattie tried to focus on the man's words of reassurance. He sounded sincere. Honest. Besides, nothing had come over his radio to refute him. Linda was strong.

Probably the strongest woman Mattie knew. She was going to be fine. She had to be. If anything happened to her, Tony would—

Tony.

Gasping, Mattie fumbled in her purse for her cell phone. Flipping open the cover, she pressed the speed dial button assigned to Tony's apartment. The phone rang three times before she abruptly hung up. She stared at the phone, second and third thoughts assailing her.

Of course Tony would want to know. He and Linda had dated for almost six months before they broke up, and she'd never seen her brother so desperately in love before. Codependent was how Linda had described it.

Should she tell him? Now? When she had no information about Linda's condition?

His emotions were still raw where Linda was concerned. The last thing he needed right now was an excuse to turn back to the drugs.

But if she didn't tell him, he'd be so angry with her. Rightfully so.

So she'd tell him, but not just yet. Not until she had more information.

Raking both hands through her hair, she stepped closer to the doors and pressed her nose against one. Her breath fogged the panel and she closed her eyes, leaning her forehead against the cool glass.

Trust Dominic, she urged herself. *He promised to come as soon as he knew something.*

She opened her eyes again and willed him to appear. When she accomplished nothing but straining her eyesight, she sank into one of the plastic chairs lining the walls and dropped her face in her hands. Just this afternoon, Linda had been flirting with Dominic, doing her best to keep his attention off Mattie. Now she was lying out in the cold, hurt.

Mattie snapped upright when she realized Linda was probably wondering where Mattie was. Why she'd left her alone.
Linda was a doer. She'd want Mattie to do something, not
stand here waiting around. The thought of failing her friend
had her pushing open the doors. The cold stung her lungs,
exacerbating her worry and dread.

"Ma'am, please—"

Moving fast, halfway to the parking garage already, Mattie
ignored Deputy O'Neil until he caught her arm, his grip sur-
prisingly firm. "Ma'am, you need to stay inside with me."

She tried to jerk away, tears of frustration forming when
he easily hung on. "Why? There are cops all over the place
now. No one's going to jump out and attack me."

The expression she'd come to know as Dom's "cop face"
formed on O'Neil's. Calm. Detached. Yet somehow demanding obedience. "Still, it's safer for all parties if the scene is
cleared."

"What parties? There's only one person out there who
matters." She pulled frantically at her arm. "I need to make
sure my friend is okay."

"Deputy Jeffries—"

"—is not calling in. My friend is—"

But O'Neil was looking over her head. She whirled around
when she heard voices and saw the gurney moving toward
them, this time with a bundled form on top of it. She ripped
away from the man holding her. "Linda!"

One of the paramedics looked up as she ran toward him.
"How is she?"

"Please, ma'am, get back—"

Mattie strained to see over the man's shoulder. She cried
out when she saw Linda's face above the sheet. Blood and
bruises stood out garishly against pasty skin. Her top lip was
split and swollen twice its size. "Linda?" she called. "Linda!"

But Linda didn't move. Didn't so much as flinch at the sound of her voice.

The men lifted the gurney into the back of the ambulance.

"Move out of the way, ma'am," one of the paramedics commanded when she blocked the closing door.

"Wait. Where are you—?"

"Mattie, let them take her to the hospital."

She jerked around at the sound of Dominic's voice. His expression was blank, revealing nothing about Linda's condition. Even though she knew she was being unfair, the expression made her furious. "I want to follow them. I want to go with her."

He nodded. "I'll take you there."

"She didn't answer when I called to her. Is she okay? Why didn't she answer?"

The ambulance motor turned over and the driver pulled away, sirens wailing.

Mattie stared at the ambulance's departing taillights in shock. She couldn't stop her teeth from chattering.

"Mattie—"

She turned on him, pushing away her fear with anger. "Why didn't you call in? Why didn't you tell me what was going on?"

"Mattie, listen to me—"

"You said you would let me know as soon as possible." She slapped his hands away when he reached for her. Her voice rose higher. "She needed me. She's probably scared. Wondering where I am. Damn you, I should have been there for her. God, I hate you! I should never have listened—"

He leaned down until his eyes were level with hers. "She was in cardiac arrest when I got to her, Mattie. I had to do CPR until the paramedics arrived, and then I needed make sure they got her safely to the ambulance. I couldn't leave them until the perimeter was cleared. I came out as soon as I could, do you understand?"

He'd done CPR on Linda? That meant her heart had stopped beating. Then, of course, getting a message to her had been the last thing he'd been worried about.

What an idiot she'd been. Raising a shaky hand to her temple, she moaned at the way she'd lost control. Yelled at him. Hit him. "I'm sorry. I—I—"

"They stabilized her, but she hasn't gained consciousness. Not since Nichols found her."

Opening her eyes, she blinked rapidly to push back the tears. "Did she talk? Did she say who did this to her?"

He pressed his lips together as if he was weighing how much to tell her. "I'll fill you in while I drive you to the hospital. Does she have family that needs to be contacted?"

She fell into step next to him, thankful for the hand he cupped under her elbow. "She has a sister in San Diego. Her mother lives back East."

"What about a brother or father? Boyfriend?"

"No brother. Her father died when she was little. And no, no boyfriend right now."

He guided her across the street, stopping at a black Durango.

"Why are you asking me about a boyfriend? Did she say something?"

"Yes, she said a name. I don't know what it means, but…."

He stared at her as his words faded. While his features remained composed, his blue eyes were filled with emotion: Regret. Compassion. And suspicion.

But that was ridiculous. Why would he be suspicious?

"What was the name?"

His hand tightened under her elbow, his touch somehow

increasing her trepidation. Instinctively, she pulled away. He scowled, but let his hand drop.

"What was the name?" she whispered.

"Tony."

Chapter 11

She'd shut down. Of course she had. He hadn't expected anything else.

As soon as he'd mentioned the name Tony, she'd stopped talking, except to tell him to bring her to the hospital. Now, as they sat in the waiting room for news about Linda, he decided he'd had enough. Placing himself directly in front of her, he held out a cup of vending machine coffee.

She glanced up, her face pale and her eyes dazed, staring at the cup as if she didn't know what it was. Sighing, Dom knelt down in front of her. He took one of her hands and wrapped her fingers around the cup, knowing the lukewarm coffee would do little to alleviate her shock.

"Have they told you anything?" she asked in the same ghostly whisper she'd used back at his truck.

"Not yet." He raised a hand and brushed the backs of his fingers against her cheek. Once more, he was struck by a feeling of rightness. When he talked to her, when he touched her, he felt calm. The restlessness that flowed through his veins seemed to subside. He wanted to bask in it, but now wasn't the time. She pulled away from his touch. The rejection stung just as much as it had before. "Don't you think it's time we talked, Mattie? If I'm going to help Linda, I need to know if this attack was personal."

She averted her eyes, but he nudged her chin up, refusing to let her hide. "She and your brother are dating?"

Biting her lip, she shook her head. "Thirsty," she murmured. He straightened and settled into the seat next to her. With a trembling hand, she raised the cup to her mouth and took a sip. "They used to date. A few years ago. But Tony didn't do this. He couldn't have."

He didn't bother telling her that anyone was capable of violence. That even seventy-year-old women had been found guilty of serial murder. She wouldn't listen to that, and it certainly wouldn't get her to open up to him. "I've never met your brother, but from the little you've told me, I'm sure he wouldn't. But I need to know why Linda said his name when she'd just been attacked. Have they talked recently?"

"No. I just saw Tony yesterday. He was over at my house, watching Jordan."

She gasped and all the color drained from her face. The hand holding her coffee jerked, spilling its contents on both his legs and hers. She didn't even notice. Fear had darkened her eyes until the brown orbs dominated her pale face. Dropping the cup on the floor, she dug into her purse.

Dom winced, knowing instantly she was looking for her cell phone. She was afraid now. Afraid for her daughter. If she was wrong, she'd regret it later, but if she was right…

He deliberately kept his voice gentle. Soothing. "Where is Jordan now?"

"At a friend's." She dialed a number, her breaths panicked. "Janet, this is Mattie Nolan, Jordan's mom. I was just checking in—" Her features and her shoulders relaxed. "Oh, a Disney movie? And they had pizza for dinner. That's great. Yes, I can hear them in the background." She glanced at Dom quickly before looking away. "I know we talked about you taking Jordan to school in the morning and I wanted to make sure that still works. A friend of mine is in the hospital and I'm not sure what's going to happen. Yes. Thank you. I appreciate it." Another glance at Dom. "Janet, I'm going to pick her up from school. Until then, if—if anyone else comes to your house for her, don't let them leave with her. And would you call me immediately on my cell number? Thank you."

She shut her phone and stared at him, refusing to meet Dom's eyes.

"Mattie—"

Her head snapped up, her eyes fierce. "I don't think he did this. But she's my daughter. I have to protect her no matter what."

Dom reached out and covered her hand, which still gripped the cell phone with whitened knuckles. The trembling he hadn't seen before tickled his palm.

"It's okay, Mattie. I understand. You're a good mother."

"You don't know anything about me," she whispered.

"I know you care about Linda. That you wouldn't let any of us stop you from checking on her. I know you care about your brother, but that some small part of you, as much as you don't want to, has reason to doubt him." Unfortunately, Dom couldn't stop pushing until he learned the reason for himself.

"Yes, but—"

"There are no buts. Once we get news about Linda, I can go check on Jordan—"

"No!"

He jerked at her vehement refusal, but she quickly shook her head. "She's perfectly fine with Janet and the school won't let her leave with anyone but me unless I call first. You need to concentrate on finding out what happened to Linda. You may not know this, but her apartment was broken into—"

"Mattie—" he began, but before he could continue a man dressed in light blue scrubs walked into the room.

He pulled down his surgical mask. "Deputy Jeffries?"

With one last piercing look at Mattie, Dom turned to the doctor. "Yes?"

"Ms. Delaney has been stabilized, but she hasn't regained consciousness yet."

Mattie stepped forward. "Is that normal?"

"You are?"

"This is Ms. Delaney's friend, Mattie Nolan."

The doctor looked at him oddly. "May I talk freely in front of her?"

Dom ran his fingers through his hair. "Yes, of course. You're free to tell her about the patient's condition."

The doctor nodded. "I'm afraid it's too soon to tell. She suffered internal bleeding, and the pressure on her brain made things tricky. Right now all we can do is wait."

Dom jolted when Mattie reached out, took his hand, and squeezed it tightly. The doctor noticed, but she seemed completely unaware of her actions. The small gesture made his chest tighten. He squeezed her hand back.

"You mean she might never wake up?" Mattie asked.

"I didn't say that. Just that it's too soon to tell. I suggest you go home for now."

"I'm not going home until I see her."

The doctor arched a brow. "I'm sorry, but visiting hours are over."

A mutinous expression took over Mattie's face. In college, it would have been impossible to find anyone with a sunnier disposition. She'd always been a force to reckon with when crossed, however. If the doctor refused to let her see Linda, they'd be here all night. "Can you make an exception?" Dom asked, although his tone indicated he expected his request to be granted. "I promise we'll be quick. It's been a difficult night for Ms. Nolan and I'm sure she'll rest easier if she can just see her friend."

The doctor hesitated, then sighed. "The guard is outside her door as you requested, Deputy. I assume you'll be accompanying Ms. Nolan?"

He squeezed her hand again when she stiffened, automatically putting the worst spin on the doctor's comment. "Yes."

"Then I'll give you five minutes. Please don't make me regret my decision by staying longer or trying to rouse the patient to ask her questions."

"Thanks, doc."

They followed him down several hallways to Linda's room, Mattie muttering all the way. "Do you think that doctor could have been more suspicious? As if I could have done that to Linda. Not to mention the fact that I was with you when it happened—" She stopped speaking so abruptly he knew she'd finally remembered their kiss.

"Yes," he agreed lightly. "You definitely were a little distracted, too."

She smiled tightly as they reached the correct room. Hands on her hips, she managed to look down her little nose at him. "I wasn't that distracted."

Dominic nodded at Deputy O'Neil before looking down at her. "That's too bad," he responded softly. "Because I definitely was." He gave himself a moment to enjoy the way her eyes widened and her lips parted before he motioned Mattie toward the room. "Go on," he said. "I'll be right here." A small smile stretched his lips when she continued to stare at him. "Five minutes, you hear? I don't want to get in trouble."

Even as he watched her open the door and slip silently inside, Dom let out a deep breath and raked his hand through his hair. One thing was for sure. He was already in trouble.

* * *

Ten minutes later, as Dominic drove Mattie home, she laid her head back on the seat, closed her eyes, and tried to block the image of Linda's still, bruised face. Even when she managed to do so, however, all she felt was guilt. Yes, her brother had acted uncharacteristically when he'd been hooked on the drugs. However, he'd never done anything to warrant Mattie's fear that he might harm Jordan.

The flash of panic had been brief, she tried telling herself. Just a few minutes. But in the end it didn't matter how brief her thoughts had been.

For those few minutes, she'd considered the possibility that Tony had hurt Linda and that he might actually pose a threat to Jordan. What did that say about her? What did that say about the world she lived in?

"You aren't different from anyone else, Mattie, so stop beating yourself up."

The husky baritone of Dominic's words penetrated her self-castigation. She raised her head and stared at his profile. His features were set in grim lines but he didn't take his eyes off the road in front of them.

"You don't understand," she began, but he didn't let her finish.

"Of course I do. You love your brother and you believe in him, but you aren't willing to take any chances, not when it comes to your daughter. That doesn't make you a bad sister, it makes you a smart mother."

"Maybe in your world it does, but in mine…" She shook her head. "Besides," she said, unable to verbalize her own disloyalty, "there are a lot of Tonys in the world. Lots, I'm sure, that Linda has prosecuted."

With a sudden jerk of the wheel, Dominic pulled the truck to the curb. A couple of teenagers walking a dog stared at them even as they continued to walk past. He turned to her, his eyes fiery enough that she instinctively flinched back. The calm mask he almost always wore was gone, replaced by a heat and intensity that was as captivating as it was scary.

"Yes, that's possible. But sometimes things aren't so complicated. Sometimes things are exactly what they first appear to be. And it appears you have reason to believe that your brother might be capable of assaulting an ex-girlfriend. I need to know why."

"So you can throw him against a table like you did Dusty?" she shot back, even as she knew she was being unfair. He'd just been doing his job then. What really bothered her was the realization that all this emotion, all this passion, was still about his job rather than her. He didn't seem the slightest bit concerned about his actions with Dusty.

"No, so I can confirm whether Linda said his name as an identification or as a warning."

"A warning?" she parroted. Confusion warred with mistrust. "Why would Linda—?"

"You tell me, Mattie."

She opened her mouth but she didn't know what he was talking about. Was he saying Linda had wanted to warn Tony that he was in danger, or that she'd wanted to warn others about Tony? Did it really matter? Either way, all roads would lead back to the one mistake Tony was struggling so hard to overcome. She wasn't saying anything that might ruin that for him.

Despite his drug history, Tony had managed to avoid the law. He'd never been arrested. Never even been questioned. For all she knew, Dominic had mentioned a warning for the sole purpose of throwing her off and making her talk.

At her stubborn silence, Dominic let out an impatient breath. "Fine. You don't want to talk about him? We have much more important things to talk about anyway. Why don't you tell me about Jordan?"

Apparently, hostile protectiveness was becoming a natural response for her. She thrust out her chin and practically dared him to push her further. "Why?"

"Because you freak out whenever I mention her," he said quietly.

She had to force herself not to wilt. "I don't freak out, but you seem to mention her a lot. Why are you so curious about her?"

"Because she's yours. And I wish she could have been ours."

Shock slammed into her like a knockout punch. For a moment, she could only stare at him while trying to keep her expression clear of longing. Then guilt. Then anger. The anger wasn't easy to suppress. How dare he say that to her? When Jordan had spent most of her life without a father— the father that would have been hers if only Dom had loved Mattie enough to stay with her.

But he hadn't.

He'd loved the idea of being a cop more than he'd loved her. If he'd ever loved her at all.

"You made your choice a long time ago, Dom. Leave me and my daughter alone. Please."

"I'm sorry," he said after several tense minutes had passed. "I know I shouldn't have said that. I guess I never thought you could hate me so much that you couldn't even tell me about your daughter."

His quiet words snuffed the anger out of her. She saw the regret on his face. Imagined that regret would magnify a thousand fold if he knew the truth. But she had no intention of telling him the truth. Ever. Dom was an upstanding public servant who hadn't even known his child existed. He could make a claim that would be hard for any judge to ignore.

She wasn't taking that chance.

Still, she thought. What harm would it do to tell him a little about Jordan?

He reached to shift the truck into Drive, but froze when Mattie began talking. "Jordan's innocent, even for her age. She sees only the goodness in people and she's stunned when anyone hurts another, especially when kids tease each other or are mean to animals."

"How old is she?"

She almost panicked, but managed to say, "She's nine. John and I... Well, part of the reason we got married so quickly after you and I—I mean, he and I... I got pregnant." There. It was the truth, even if it was designed to misdirect him.

His mouth twisted. "And we were always so careful about using protection."

She turned and stared straight ahead, wondering if she was imagining the hurt in his voice. Yes, they'd always used protection, but her body had found a way to work around that.

He sighed. "Sorry. I didn't mean to make that sound like an accusation. So Jordan... You were saying she's sensitive?"

Mattie hesitated, then cleared her throat. "Extremely so. But she's not shy or quiet either. She's loud—far louder than most of her classmates—and adventurous. Again, more than other girls her age. She's why I tried that rock-climbing class, and she wants to kayak next."

"But? Because I can hear the but in your voice." Carefully, he pulled back on the road.

"But—I—I'm still scared of the water. I never learned to swim."

"I remember that."

"I've taken lessons time and again. My body's just not made for swimming."

"Maybe it's made for other things."

The innuendo, said so calmly, caused the heat, which had

been set to simmer ever since he'd kissed her, to flame wildly. "Uh, I—"

He shook his head. "Sorry, I couldn't help myself."

Mattie looked out the passenger window. As Dominic turned into her neighborhood, she remembered the day she and John had moved into the little house she loved. She'd thought she'd found it then—a man in uniform who loved his job but loved her more. Loved her enough to give her the security and stability she and her little girl needed. Instead, he'd thrown it all away for thrills.

Dom pulled up to the curb outside her house and stopped. She reached for the handle of the door, but then hesitated. She stared at her little house, with all the windows dark, and thought how lonely it looked without Jordan's presence to light it up. Her daughter was quickly growing up and would eventually be moving out on her own. And then what would Mattie have waiting at home for her? An empty house, as empty as she felt right at that moment.

Empty. Aching. Lonely.

And damn it, she didn't want to be empty any longer. She wanted to be filled up. Just for a little while, she wanted to forget the past few days and just feel again.

She fell back against her seat, closed her eyes, and dropped her head back. Minutes passed and the whole time she felt the heavy caress of Dom's gaze. "I don't want to go inside," she whispered. Turning her head, she opened her eyes and saw desire tighten his features. "Isn't that crazy? I've done nothing but push you away since you came back into my life and now, after one lousy dinner and ride home, despite the horrible things that have happened tonight, I don't want to leave you. How can you have such power over me, Dom?"

Reaching out, he cupped her face. "I don't know, but you've got the same hold on me, Mattie. I swear."

"I can't talk about Tony. I won't—"

Catching her in his arms, he pulled her close, rested his chin on the top of her head, and wrapped his arms around her. "Then don't. Not tonight. Tonight, let me just be with you. Let someone—let *me*—take care of you for once, Mattie."

She closed her eyes and breathed him in. Felt herself relax, as if his nearness was a drug, wiping away all her fears and doubts. After a moment, she pulled away from him. "Come in." She tried to open the door, but he stayed her with a hand on her arm.

"Wait." He looked torn, even as desire made his cheeks flush and his nostrils flare. "No misunderstandings, Mattie. First I want you to tell me exactly what you want."

She frowned. "You—you know what I want."

He shook his head and soothed a hand over her shoulder in a calming motion. "Your friend's been hurt. You're worried about your brother. I know you want comfort, but we don't need to have sex for me to give you that. If you want me to hold you, I'll hold you, nothing else. But if you want more, I need to know it's because you want *me*, me inside you, and not just anyone would do."

"That's crazy!" She made a frustrated noise deep in her throat and stared out the window again. "Why does it matter, anyway? I bet you didn't ask that girl who left naked pictures for you whether she wanted you or just physical release, now did you?"

He sighed and turned her face back toward him. "It didn't matter with her. It does with you."

She tried to turn away, but he only held her firmer. "I'm not saying it has to mean more than tonight. We have a hell of a past, one too complicated for talk of the future right now. But I need to know it's me you want."

When she didn't respond, he released her and sat back. Somehow, what he was asking seemed more than she could give and she felt indecision creeping in.

"You know," he said, "those naked pictures were a turn-on because of the sentiment behind them, not just because they showed some T and A."

The statement shocked her out of her thoughts. "What sentiment?" she snorted. "The 'I'm yours, you can do anything you want to me, just do me now' sentiment?"

"Exactly."

She laughed uncomfortably. "At least you're honest. So what's your point? Men like total subjugation in a woman? Is that what you're asking for?"

"Not subjugation. Total passion. Total focus. Total commitment. That woman wanted me and she wanted me so bad that she was willing to put herself on the line to get me. That's what really turns a man on. Not a woman with the best technique or the most moves, but the woman who's so overcome by passion, *her* passion, that she'll forget about her inhibitions. Screw propriety. Screw what other people think. She wants him and she's going to take him. You gave me that once, Mattie, and I want it again. Despite our past. Despite the bad timing. I need you to say it and mean it."

"You're twisted," she breathed.

"Am I? Tell me the truth. It wouldn't turn you on—to drive me crazy with lust, to know that I ache for you, long for your touch, dream about your body under mine, to the point that all I can think, speak, or breathe is you? That I would do anything to have you? That with one word, you can heighten my suffering or end it simply by teasing me or giving me everything I've ever wanted? Because that's how it is. How it's always been with you, Mattie. I look at you and I want you."

She was breathing hard, staring at him as if she'd never seen him before. Opening her mouth, she tried to speak but couldn't. Instead, she opened the door, slipped out, and bent down to meet his eyes.

"I want to have sex with you," she said, her voice measured. "You, Dom, and no one else. So, please, come in."

She saw the flash of surprise on his face, but didn't wait to see more. Slamming the truck door shut, she moved up the walk, her breaths escalating when she heard him get out of the truck and follow her.

What was she doing? Was she crazy? The man was Jordan's father. He had reason to believe Tony had attacked Linda. And he'd hurt her. God, he'd hurt her. But despite all that, she still wanted him to stay. She—

She gasped when he caught her arm.

Praying he wasn't dreaming, Dom bent and gave Mattie the briefest of kisses before pulling back. He leaned in for more less than two seconds later, rubbing their mouths together and licking at the seam of her lips in a silent plea for entry. She gasped and opened her mouth, inviting him in. He took the invitation for what it was. Something unexpected and precious.

Fighting for control, he forced himself to be gentle. To go slow. He rubbed his tongue against hers, encouraging her to do the same. She tasted like brandied apricots, sweet but with a definite kick, and he opened his mouth wider, loosening his control by degrees as she followed his lead. Soon, their combined breaths echoed around them and he pulled back. For a moment, her mouth blindly sought his until she blinked her eyes rapidly and stepped back.

Turning towards the door, she shakily inserted the key while he caressed her shoulders and back, unable to keep his hands off her. Which is why he felt her stiffen. She stared at her hand poised in front of the lock.

"Mattie, what is it?"

She released the key and stumbled back, bumping into him. "I locked it. I know I did. But it's already unlocked."

Taking in her words along with the paleness of her complexion, Dom immediately put himself in front of her. "Go next door and call 911."

"What are you doing?" she hissed even as she clung to his arm and pulled him back. "How do you know someone's not inside?"

"I'm a cop, Mattie. If someone's inside, I'll deal with it. Now go."

She stared at him with true fear in her eyes, but then she turned and ran away. He waited until she was out of sight before he drew his gun from his holster and carefully pushed her front door open.

The entry was dark. Although he felt along the wall for a light switch, there wasn't one. Cursing, he realized that because the house was older, the rooms were probably illuminated by lamps rather than overhead lighting. Sure enough, a small fussy lamp with a green, beaded shade sat on the entry table.

The end of the foyer led into some kind of family room/kitchen combination, with another open doorway to the right. Keeping his back to the wall, he moved silently forward, keeping his gun steady. Cautiously, he searched the shadows for movement but there was none.

Room by room, he searched the house, but if anyone had been there, they'd gone. The place hadn't been ransacked, but he couldn't know if anything was missing until Mattie came back. Snatching the kitchen phone from its receiver, he called dispatch and confirmed that officers were on their way. He hung up, then headed toward the front door to wait for Mattie. The small foyer table was piled high with files and papers, and, as he passed it, he accidentally knocked some papers and a picture frame over. He straightened the picture frame. When he saw the picture it contained, his mind went numb.

Despite the possible threat of Mattie's intruders returning, shock got the better of him. Knees wobbling, he felt so dizzy he had to reach out a hand to steady himself on the table.

Jordan Nolan had dark curly hair just like Mattie, but she had blue eyes. A bright blue that could have rivaled his. And where Mattie's face was rounded, Jordan's was oval, with high angular cheekbones and a slight cleft chin. All in all, except for her hair, Jordan Nolan looked just like her father.

She looked like him.

The door creaked open and Dom whirled around, his gun up and ready.

Mattie.

She was staring at him, her hand covering her mouth and tears shining in her eyes. Immediately lowering his gun, he vaguely thought that she shouldn't be here. That she should have waited for the police to arrive before entering the house. But nothing seemed to matter at the moment but getting her to admit what he knew to be true.

"Mattie?" His voice trembled. "Mattie, is she mine?"

"No." She shook her head violently. "She's mine, Dominic. Just mine."

One hand still gripping the gun, he reached out with his free hand to take her arm. Ever aware of his greater strength, he forced himself to be gentle despite the riotous emotions swirling inside him. "Damn you, don't play games now. Not now. Her eyes...I know she's mine, but I assumed—you *let* me assume—she was conceived after I left."

She tried to pull away, but he wouldn't let her. "That's right, Dom, you left. You didn't want anything to do with me."

He dropped his hand. He wanted to deny her accusation, but knew he couldn't. "If I'd known—"

"What? You would have stayed? I suspected as much, but no thank you."

Nine years. He'd lost nine years with Mattie and his little girl, who'd been claimed by someone else.

"Think about it, Dom. Your priority was to be a cop, regardless of my concerns. I didn't want a man tied to me because of a baby. If you stayed out of obligation, you really would have ended up hating me."

He shook his head, denying her words. Obligation? More like an inescapable reason to ignore his fears. To take the risk he'd been too much of a coward to take. But in a way, she'd been a coward, too. She'd taken the choice away from him. "You should have told me. You should have—"

They heard the sirens just before the police cars pulled up in front of the house. Dominic pulled out his badge to show the responding officers, but not before he turned to Mattie. Gripping her chin, he bent down to give her a quick, hard kiss. The anger was there, but crowded along with it was possessiveness. Even joy. He just didn't know what to do with either one. With his face close to hers, he warned, "She's mine. And this isn't over, Mattie. Not by a long shot."

Chapter 12

Dom wasn't angry, he was royally pissed. Someone was playing with Mattie, rifling through her purse, coming into her home, obviously trying to scare her. But for what purpose? And would the threats continue until they finally became more? Until danger touched Mattie and her daughter?

Their little girl, he reminded himself, still trying to accept it.

He looked at Mattie, who was speaking to the responding officers. She was pale, her features pinched and anxious, and she deliberately avoided looking at him. Although she hadn't admitted Jordan was his, he didn't doubt it nor did he doubt that as soon as the police left, they were going to have it out. Anticipating that conversation filled him with both satisfaction and dread. He knew he'd ultimately get the truth out of her, but with it he'd also get the fury and sadness that had been building in the past ten years.

Restlessly, he moved through her house, taking in the cheery but functional furniture. Most of all, he examined the pictures in frames and on the walls. Pictures of his little girl. All the moments in time that he'd missed and could never get back. Her baby phase when she was all fleshy rolls and gummy smiles. Her sulky toddler phase, with her hair in pigtails and gaps between her teeth. Jordan in her peewee softball uniform. Dressed in a pink tutu. At the zoo. Picture after picture of her with Mattie and with other men. A man he knew had to be her brother, Tony. And another man whose blue uniform proclaimed him to be the infamous John Nolan.

The picture that floored him, however, was a black-and-white Mattie had hung on a wall between the living room and her kitchen. It was a five-by-seven of her in full pregnancy, about ready to pop. It was Mattie just months after he'd left her, beaming at the camera. While he couldn't see the man who stood out of the camera's range, the man's hand rested protectively on Mattie's bulging belly.

Mine, he thought. *That should have been my hand. On my baby. On my Mattie.*

But she'd kept it all from him. Her pregnancy. His daughter's birth.

For a moment, he directed all the anger he felt for her stalker towards Mattie. At least he tried to. The anger faltered and redirected before it could even get started. Dropping his face into his hands, he faced the truth.

As much as he wanted to blame Mattie—as much as he wanted to hate her for what she'd done—he knew the blame lay with him.

Mattie had once offered him everything. Herself. Children. A home. He could have had his daughter. Instead, he'd given it all up. For what? For adrenaline, just as Mattie had said?

If so, that meant the last ten years of his life had been not only a mistake, but completely worthless. He just couldn't accept that.

No. He'd become who he needed to be. He'd followed who he really was. And in doing so, he'd done some good.

He still had good to do. He needed to solve this case. Find Joel's killer. And of more importance now, find out who was threatening Mattie and put a stop to it.

And then what? He didn't know what would change if he could give Mattie what she needed. But he'd protect her and Jordan with his life if he had to.

One officer signaled to him and he stepped close to Mattie, deliberately brushing up against her, then putting a proprietary arm around her waist. She stiffened, but didn't pull away.

"As I was telling Ms. Nolan, there's not much we can do. There's no visible signs of forced entry. Nothing has been stolen or damaged. We've processed the front door for prints, but—" The officer shrugged, clearly communicating his belief that no relevant prints would be found.

"What about a patrol car? Can you have someone drive by to check on her?"

"I don't need—" Mattie began, stopping when Dom glared at her.

"I didn't ask what you needed, Mattie. I asked what the police could do."

She narrowed her eyes and pulled away from him, striding into the kitchen and grabbing her phone off the receiver. The officer cleared his throat, pulling Dom's attention back to him.

"Though there's no real reason to connect this with Ms. Delaney's attack, given you're a fellow officer and this lady obviously means something to you, I'll do my best to make sure she gets some coverage. But based on what we know, it's not going to be much and it's not going to last very long. I'm sorry, but we just don't have the resources to—"

Dom nodded. "Thank you. I appreciate whatever you can

do." He appreciated it, but it wasn't enough. Given what happened to Joel and given that Frank Manelli was still missing, Dom wasn't taking any chances with Mattie or Jordan.

Apparently, she wasn't willing to take any chances with her daughter, either.

As the police left, he propped himself on the counter next to her, arms crossed over his chest, blatantly listening to her telephone conversation.

"Yes, it's going to be great, Jordan. I'm glad the idea of staying with your grandparents makes you happy. I just talked to them and they're thrilled to see you." Mattie's eyes locked on Dom's. He cocked one brow, making her flush and turn away.

"I'll pick you up at school tomorrow and drive you to your grandparents' house." She laughed hollowly, then stuttered, "M-me? I'll be fine, sweetie. No. No, I won't be alone. I mean, I'll miss you, but I have lots to catch up with. Okay, I'll see you tomorrow."

She hung up the phone, but kept her back to Dom.

"Since I remember your parents are dead, I'm guessing you're close to your in-laws?"

Her finger began to trace the grout between the kitchen counter tiles. "I'm not as close, but they do care for Jordan, in a bit of a distant way. They live in a very secure, gated community. They'll take care of her."

He moved closer until he bumped up against her back. Gently, he placed his hands on her shoulders. "And who's going to take care of you?"

Swiftly, she turned and placed one of her dining room chairs between them. "I don't need anyone to take care of me. I can take care of myself."

"Good. I'm glad that's settled."

She scowled. "Meaning?"

"Meaning, you can come back to my place or I can take you to a hotel. Either way, you're not going to stay here."

"That's exactly what I'm going to do."

He talked right over her. "Why don't you get your things and tomorrow I can drive you to pick up Jordan—"

"You're not driving me anywhere, and you're not getting anywhere near my daughter."

"Our daughter," he reminded her.

"Biology doesn't negate ten years of absence."

"Of course it does, since I never even knew she existed. You kept me from her, Mattie."

"You got what you really wanted. You became a cop."

"I want to see her," Dom said. "I will see her. Even if I have to get a court order to do so."

She jerked back as if he'd slapped her. He hated the fear that so starkly radiated from her at that moment. "I'm not going to take her from you, Mattie," he said softly. "But I do need to see her. I'm trained to protect people. She won't be safer with anyone than she would be with me."

Talking about Jordan's safety seemed to do the trick. Mattie swallowed hard, then shrugged. "Fine. You can pick me up tomorrow. We'll get her together, but you can't say anything to her. About…you know."

"No. I don't know. You mean about me being her real father? Or about you deciding that wasn't important enough to tell either of us?"

She looked away. "She's a happy little girl, Dom. You can't—"

"I won't, Mattie. Not yet. But someday? I'm not making any guarantees. Now let's get going."

Again, she shook her head, making him furious. "I'm staying here. There's no reason to think that whoever was here will come back or that they mean me any harm. They didn't destroy anything or take anything. Heck, maybe I'm being a fool and I simply forgot to lock the door after all."

"You don't believe that."

"No," she said, her mouth twisting regretfully. "I don't. But I'm not spending the night anyplace else but my home."

He didn't bother to hide his frustration. "I have to work, Mattie. I can't stay with you."

"I didn't ask you to."

He stared at her. At the stubborn, defiant expression on her face. She'd fight him if he tried to make her leave. And what good would that do them? She was right. There was no solid evidence that she was in danger. Still…

"Your brother," he clipped out. "Does he have a key to your house?"

She didn't answer for a moment. When she did, she just nodded, her eyes daring him to anything about it.

Instead, he said, "I'll be back in five minutes."

"Wait! What—"

He took off in his truck and drove straight to a hardware store. Minutes later, he was back with what he needed. If little Ms. Independent didn't like it, that was too bad. She obviously watched out for her friends and family. She could let someone watch out for her for a change.

Sure enough, she tried blocking his entry by standing in the doorway. He merely held up the plastic bag. "I'm going to change your locks. Unless you think you can actually get to sleep knowing someone out there might have a copy of your key?"

Biting her lip, she stared at the bag. Then with another shrug, she took several steps back. "Thank you," she muttered.

He changed the locks with stiff, jerky movements, acutely aware of her eyes on him. When he was done, he stood, wiped his hands on the towel she offered, then handed it back to her. Prowling from one room to the next, he checked to make sure that every window and door was locked. "I'll see you in the morning," he said finally.

When he turned to leave, he felt her hand on his shoulder. She wouldn't be able to miss the frustration vibrating through him.

"I did what I thought was best for all of us, Dom."

He didn't turn toward her. He drank in her touch and tried to imagine how she'd felt when she'd learned she was pregnant, knowing that her baby's father had just walked out on her. He couldn't be angry with her for not telling him. Not then. And not now. But that didn't mean he was going to let things continue the way they had been.

"I know that. And I'm going to do the same, Mattie." He started down the walk.

"Is that a threat?"

He stopped and turned, gave her a wolfish grin, and winked at her. "That's a promise, babe."

In the squad room an hour later, Dom threw his pencil down and ran his hands wearily through his hair. He'd wanted to stay and protect Mattie, but she wouldn't have allowed it. He thought he could do more by solving the case. He'd gone through the evidence over and over again in his head. Linda's assault. The subtle threats against Mattie. There was more to them than a cheating spouse trying to cover his ass, even if that spouse was a public official. It all had to lead back to Joel and Guapo. Probably Manelli as well.

There had been no word from Manelli. No sign of foul play, nothing to indicate that he hadn't just up and disappeared to start a new life and avoid having to pay his soon-to-be ex-wife alimony payments.

Obviously, Guapo was of no help. He'd just gotten word that the bastard had attacked his cell mate and landed himself in solitary. Days before, when a prison guard had asked him about Joel Bustamante and Frank Manelli, Guapo had simply laughed. Even if he had the man in front of him, even with all his skill in interrogating witnesses, Dom wasn't so sure he could refrain from strangling him long enough to get the information he needed. But then again, he knew no matter how skilled he was, questioning Guapo wouldn't get him the answers he needed. Mattie's brother Tony had to be key, but he hadn't learned anything useful about him, not from her, the police databases, or from the neighbors he'd interviewed. As far as everyone knew, Tony Cooper was a saint among men, and that right there was a sure sign of trouble. Dominic turned to Cameron, who was steadfastly reading something on his computer screen. "What's been the department gossip about Joel? Is there still talk of suicide?"

"No one's stupid enough to say it out loud, but there's still speculation. With the brass. The new shrink. Internal Affairs."

Dom snorted. "How's that for gratitude. Joel was a poster boy for this office, good enough to promote to sergeant but at the slightest hint of trouble—" Dom pounded his fist on his desk, rattling pens and several empty coffee cups.

"It's tough adjusting to the real world, isn't it? Where the things we do don't seem to make a difference and sometimes the bad guys live better than a cop ever can."

Cam's sarcastic reply caught Dom unaware. He stared at the man. "What's that supposed to mean?"

Leaning back in his chair, the tall Brit shrugged. "No offense, but maybe you've forgotten how things work around here, Dom. You don't believe it, and neither do I, but based on the objective evidence, Joel committing suicide because he was on the take isn't a completely bogus theory. And—" he interrupted before Dom could rise to his feet "—before you think about plastering me again, I want to reiterate that

I don't believe it. But people have jobs to do, and that means following the evidence until it can be disproved."

Dom forced his tense muscles to relax. He remembered what he'd told Mattie—that sometimes the most obvious answer *was* the answer. "What exactly do you think needs to be disproved?"

"You were on assignment for a long time, Dom. You weren't around when Joel took over, and you weren't around to see that something was bothering him the week before he died. I tried to talk to him about it, but he dug in. Said he couldn't talk until he knew for sure."

Dom stroked his chin. "The last time we talked, Joel said he had a feeling that something was wrong with the warrant Manelli wrote up for the Guapo raid. Who signed the warrant? Judge Butler. He also thought Guapo's attorney might have been killed with the help of someone in Judge Butler's chambers. What if the thing he wasn't sure about was Judge Butler's involvement in something nasty?" It wasn't that far of a stretch. The question was whether he would stoop to using Mattie's brother to do his dirty work for him.

"Could be. Given who the judge's friends are, Joel wouldn't have wanted to say anything until he was sure. But what about the warrant Manelli wrote? You got it?"

"Yeah." Dom flipped through several stacks of paper on his desk before handing Cam the warrant. "I've been over it. It looks clean. A confidential informant from within Guapo's organization made a deal to avoid doing hard time on another case and gave up the details of an upcoming buy. That in turn led to the tossing of one of Guapo's main drug labs."

"And the CI's identity?" Cam asked as his gaze ran down the warrant.

"Sealed and confidential. I don't even know if Manelli knows his real name."

"You're assuming it's a man?"

"Well, I—" Stunned, Dom stared at the warrant. "I just assumed—but you're right. It very well could be a woman."

"Pretty articulate informant, don't you think?"

The careful way Cam made the statement immediately raised Dom's antennae. "What do you mean?"

"Look, you guys are always giving me crap about my background and my accent, right? Well, look at the portions in this affidavit that Manelli attributes to the informant. Sounds a little well-educated for a common thug to be using, don't you think?"

"Give me that." Dom stared at the affidavit, took out a pencil, and started circling. "You're right. It almost sounds like legalese. Like someone who's been working in the law for awhile."

"Right. So what if someone called Manelli under the guise of being part of Guapo's organization. He—or she—had insider information and for whatever reason wanted Guapo brought down."

"But how would Judge Butler have that kind of information?"

"Maybe he wouldn't. But maybe someone on his staff would. Anyone on his staff strike you as particularly smart?"

Mattie, Dom thought automatically. *She's smart. Records legalese all the time.* She'd be familiar with the terms. With the process. And maybe she had a reason to want Guapo brought down. A personal reason having to do with her brother?

He'd already searched the computers for his name and the guy had never been arrested let alone convicted. But that didn't mean he hadn't been using or selling drugs that Guapo had supplied.

"Then again, this could all be nothing. Could be Manelli is smarter than we give him credit for and simply substituted his own words for that of the CI."

Unlike Cam, Dom had never had reason to question Manelli's intelligence. "So what's the news on Manelli?"

Cam turned back to his computer screen. "It's Lewis's case. I wasn't friends with the guy."

No, the two of them had never been friends, and everyone in the office knew why. Cam hadn't liked the way Manelli ran around on his wife. And Manelli hadn't liked Cam's obvious attraction to her.

"Have you paid her a visit yet?"

Cam's fingers stilled above the computer keyboard. "Yeah. She told me to get lost."

Dom winced. "I'm sorry, man."

Cam shrugged. "I've got a date this weekend who's more than willing to make me feel better. I can ask her to bring a friend along, if you're of a mind."

"No, but thanks for the second eye on the warrant. I'll check it out." Dom reached for the phone and dialed the county jail.

"Deputy Miller."

"Hey, Ron. This is Dominic Jeffries at Sacramento PD."

"Hey, L.B."

"L.B."—short for "Lover Boy." Dom winced at the unwanted moniker. He'd known Ron Miller for years, and for some reason the guy had gotten it into his head that Dom was some kind of stud. Of course, it hadn't helped that Dom was a serial dater. He satisfied his body when he needed to, but not since Mattie had he ever been tempted to form more than a physical relationship with a woman. Ron was a dedicated bachelor committed to putting as many notches in his bedpost as possible. He always called Dominic "L.B." with a hint of admiration and jealousy in his voice, even though his own conquests likely had reached triple figures.

"Heard you were pulling bailiff duty for awhile. How they hanging?"

"Off center at the moment."

Cam snorted behind him.

"Anything I can do to help with that?"

"I need to schedule an appointment with one of your inmates. A follow-up interview with Dusty Monroe. You know him?"

"Yep. I heard he caused some trouble for you and Pete the other day."

"You talk to Pete about it?"

"Overheard him some. He had a few choice words to say about you."

I bet he did. "Anything you want to share?"

Miller chortled. "I think you can use your imagination. Pete deserved a slap down from IA. He's been too sloppy for years. But he's not a murderer."

Dom tensed. "Who's saying he is?"

"Apparently not you, since you're calling for old Dusty."

"Tell me," Dom snapped.

"He's dead, Dom. Got hold of some bad stuff and overdosed in his cell. The solicitor general and IA are checking into it. And given what Pete's spouting off, I think they'll be giving you a call sooner than later."

Right. Dusty would've blabbed about the deputy that had threatened him, but Dom didn't feel a hint of unease. Not for himself, anyway. He'd meant every word when he'd warned Dusty not to go near Mattie again.

"What about Martin Johnson, the inmate he was transported with? Was he anywhere in the vicinity when this overdose occurred?"

"He was searched and his cell was tossed right after we got your report. We didn't find anything. His attorney bailed him out within hours after that. He's out of here."

Damn, there went his best chance for information about why Dusty had bolted into the courtroom that day. And, he'd bet, any chance of finding the person who'd given Dusty the means to overdose in his own cell.

"I need his attorney's number."

"You're smoking something if you think he'll let you talk to the guy."

"I hear you. But Johnson's connected to a few things I'm looking into. If and when I can connect the dots, I want to have Johnson's attorney on speed dial."

Chapter 13

Friday

The night of Linda's assault had been a sleepless one for Mattie. After checking and rechecking that Jordan was okay, she'd spent the hours staring at her bedroom ceiling, reliving Linda's injuries as well as the fear she'd felt when she'd believed a stranger had entered her house. She'd tried to distract herself with housework or catching up with work or updating the photos in Jordan's scrapbook, but when she wasn't thinking of Linda, her thoughts would inevitably turn to Dominic.

The first time she'd seen him in court. His kiss. His stunned acceptance when he'd learned he'd fathered a child. His silent yet determined resolve to change her locks.

His kiss.

The few times she was able to fall asleep, her dreams were haunted by images of combined violence and sensuality, jerking her awake time and again. She was nodding off when the phone rang, but she immediately answered. "Hello?"

"Mattie, it's Brenda Florentine."

"Brenda?" Mattie sat up, checked the clock, and saw it was only 9:00 a.m. She wasn't scheduled to be in court until 11:00 a.m. today.

"We heard about what happened to Linda. It's the talk of the courthouse. How is she?"

"I—I—" Mattie rubbed her eyes, trying to get her thoughts together. What was she supposed to say and not say? "She was hurt pretty badly but she's stable. I haven't gotten any more information. Does the judge know?"

"Yes. He's arranged for another court reporter to sub for you today."

"What? Why?" Annoyance tinged her voice at his presumptuousness. Since when did he make decisions like that without consulting her? And why? So she'd be away from the courthouse? So he could have someone attack her like Linda?

Slamming her hand on the mattress, Mattie ordered herself to stop it. What kind of crazy thought was that? She was letting Dominic's suspicions infect her.

"He's gotten it into his head that with the assault you suffered in court combined with this, you need some time off. You know the judge. He's always looking out for you."

Brenda's final sentence was said with a decided edge that immediately made Mattie frown. "Judge Butler is kind to all his employees. You should know that more than anyone."

The silence on the line told Mattie her barb had struck home.

"You've got him fooled, Mattie. He thinks you're so sweet, when really you're—"

"Thanks for passing along the message," she said.

There was a brief moment of silence, then Brenda snorted. "Whatever. By the way," Brenda chirped. "I have your hairbrush. I forgot to put it back in your purse after I borrowed it the other day."

The first thing Mattie felt was outrage. She'd never given Brenda permission to go into her purse. "Is my hairbrush the only thing you took?" she blurted out.

"Excuse me?"

"Someone came into my house yesterday, Brenda. Whoever it was had a key. Do you know anything about that?"

"You're crazy," Brenda shot back. "What would I want from your house? I told you, I only borrowed your hairbrush."

She hesitated, wanting to ask her what she'd done all day, but feared coming off as a hysterical fool. What possible reason would Brenda have for coming into her house, especially when nothing was taken? She obviously didn't care who knew she was seeing Judge Butler, so silencing Mattie couldn't be a motive. Annoyed with the woman and herself, she said, "Just keep it, Brenda," before hanging up.

Mattie dressed quickly and called the hospital, only to confirm that Linda's condition hadn't changed. She took a moment to assess the situation and what she should do next. Normally, the first person she'd call for legal advice after Linda was Judge Butler. Now, that wasn't even an option. She didn't believe Judge Butler had hired Tony to hurt Linda any more than she believed Tony was capable of such violence. Still, she also couldn't shake the image of Tony's face when she'd handed him Judge Butler's envelope, or his questions about whether the judge had been acting differently.

She'd tried calling Tony last night but he hadn't been home and hadn't returned any of the messages she'd left on his voice mail. She needed to talk with him first, needed to get them both to an attorney, before she decided what, if anything, to tell Dominic about his background.

She jumped when someone knocked on her door. Cursing

her nerves, she checked the peephole, then let out a sigh of relief.

Tony. Thank God.

She threw open the door and launched herself at her brother.

He staggered back with a small laugh, dropping the brown paper bag he'd been holding.

"Whoa, whoa. I'm glad you're happy to see me but—"

"Tony, I tried calling you last night. Where were you?"

He pulled away, his face overcome by concern. "What's wrong? Is something wrong with Jordan?"

The tears she'd been holding back could no longer be contained. She sobbed, racked so hard by fear and grief that she could barely breathe let alone talk. "Jordan's fine," she choked out, "but Linda—Linda—"

Tony's fingers tightened painfully on her arms. "What about Linda?"

Mattie fought to regain her composure. "She was—she was attacked last night in the parking garage at work."

The moment she said the words, she knew. Tony hadn't had anything to do with hurting Linda. She'd known him her whole life, and the shock and fear on his face was as real as it had been twelve years ago when she'd told him their parents had died in a car accident. He paled and swayed, throwing them both off balance. Mattie caught him.

"Is she—?"

"She's in the hospital. She hasn't woken up. But she—she almost died, Tony."

Tony's mouth tightened and he suddenly straightened. Looking around first, he shepherded her off the porch. "Let's go inside."

Leaning against him, she walked inside and collapsed on the couch.

He sat beside her and took her hands. "What do you mean,

she was attacked? Did anyone see who did it? Were you with her?"

"No. I was walking to the garage when I heard glass break and a car alarm go—"

Tony dropped her hands to run his through his hair. Vaguely, she noted that he'd gotten a haircut since they'd last talked. The curls she'd admired the other day had been shorn close to his head. "You were walking to the garage alone? Why weren't you together?"

"She'd left court early. And I was walking to the garage with a deputy."

His eyes sharpened. "The deputy you told me about?"

"Yes."

"Did he help her?"

"Yes. But Tony…he's asking questions about you. Linda— Linda passed out right after they found her, but not before she said your name."

Tony looked poleaxed. "My name?"

"Yes. I know she could have been talking about someone else, but did you go see her? After she dropped me—"

Another knock at the door had her jumping. She grabbed Tony's shirt front, fear suddenly making her panic. "Don't answer it."

Tony grabbed her hands and rubbed them between his. "What's going on, Mattie?"

"Mattie, it's Dominic. I know you're inside and I'm not leaving until you answer the door."

"Dominic. Wasn't that the name of the guy you—" Tony narrowed his eyes. "Who does he think he is, talking to you like that?" Tony surged to his feet and strode toward the door. She swiftly followed behind him, clinging to the back of his shirt like a monkey.

"Ignore him, Tony!"

He whirled around but gently held her away from him. "Why? I don't have anything to hide, Mattie."

Something must have flickered across her face because Tony suddenly frowned. "But apparently you think I do." Hurt shone in his eyes. "Mattie, you don't think—?" he whispered.

The pounding on the door got louder. "Mattie, are you talking to someone?"

Tony backed away from her, no longer heading for the front door but away from it.

"You do. You think I hurt Linda." He looked around. "Where's Jordan? Do you think I'd hurt her too?"

"Open the door or I'm coming in. Now."

"No, Tony, please. Just wait. I'm sorry."

"Stand back from the door. I'm coming in...."

"Tony, just wait..." Mattie ran for the door and threw it open. Dominic looked grim, muscles tense and pumped. In his hand, he grasped the paper bag that Tony had dropped. She immediately turned back to her brother. "Tony—"

But he was gone. She heard the back door of the kitchen slam and tried to go after him, but strong fingers wrapped around her arm.

"You're not going anywhere."

Dom barely moved out of the way before Mattie's fist whizzed by his temple.

They stared at one another in shock.

Narrowing his eyes, he easily picked her up, the paper bag still clutched in his hand, and kicked the door closed with his leg. He started to put her down, but Mattie went ballistic.

She started wriggling, his hardness rubbing against her soft curves even as she tried to gouge his eyes out. "Let me go!"

"Stop it," he shouted, catching both her wrists in one hand and lifting her off her feet again. He carried her over to the couch and pinned her down with his body across her chest, careful not to put his full weight on her. The care he took made her angrier and she kicked out until he pinned down her legs just in time to stop what surely would have been a debilitating blow. "Will you calm down?"

"How dare you come in here and start manhandling me? How dare you threaten to kick my door down?"

She ripped one wrist out of his grasp, but he simply caught it again and slammed both wrists down, one on either side of her head. "I thought you were in danger," he shouted.

She froze. Their breaths mingled as they stared at one another, her racing heartbeat thumping against his own. His blond hair had fallen into his eyes during their tussle and she suddenly realized that as light as his hair was, his lashes were dark fringes that framed the blue of his eyes until they shone like a beacon. "I was worried when I changed your locks. I was worried when I left. And I've been worried ever since. You think I like imagining you alone here, someone doing to you what he did to Linda?"

His genuine concern stunned her and caused an odd ache to form in her chest. She licked her lips and his eyes followed the movement as if hypnotized.

"Get off me," she whispered.

He did, slowly releasing her wrists as if anticipating her lunging for him. He held out a hand, which she ignored.

"There was a paper bag on the walkway with its contents spilled out. I heard you talking to someone in here. You sounded upset. I wasn't taking any chances."

"You know I have cause to be upset."

"That's why I gave you a few seconds. Believe me, I wouldn't have waited otherwise."

Mattie actually sneered at him. "It must be great, being big and strong enough to go wherever you want, whenever you want to."

"Yeah, well, sometimes it's not all it's cracked up to be."

He rubbed his side absently as if it suddenly pained him. When she saw her watching him, however, he dropped his hand and sat back. "Your brother ran."

Standing, she straightened her clothes, then glared at him. "Of course he did. With a crazed cop out to get him, what other choice did he have?"

Hands on hips, Dom thrust his face close to hers. "If I'm crazed, it's because you're making me that way. When are you going to get it through your head that I am not trying to hurt you?"

"No," she shot back. "You're just trying to pin my brother for attempted murder. It's been a slow week, after all."

"You have a smart mouth, Mattie, and one of these days it's going to get you into trouble."

She narrowed her eyes. "Did you just threaten me?"

He smiled tightly. "Why, yes. I do believe I did. And what are you going to do about it?"

She placed her hands on his chest and shoved. He didn't move, which made her scream in fury. She pressed her hands against him again, but this time he caught her wrists, holding her palms against hard, warm muscles. "I—I—"

"Tell me what you're going to do, Mattie," he taunted.

"Let go of my hands."

He didn't look like he was going to comply. He stared at her mouth as if he wanted to kiss her. As if he wanted to devour her. Her breath caught just as he released her hands. "Fine, but you can tell—"

Before he could step back, Mattie reached up, grabbed his ears, and pulled his head down even as she rose on her tiptoes to kiss him.

Every cell in Dom's body seemed to freeze as Mattie's lips touched his. Despite the aggression in her grasp and in her eyes, her lips were soft. Hesitant. Almost shy.

As if unsure of their welcome.

With his own breaths echoing in his ear, he watched her pull back to stare at him with dazed eyes.

"You shouldn't have done that, Mattie," he whispered.

Heat suffused her cheeks and she shook her head. "I'm sor—"

His mouth swept in, taking hers with the confidence that had been lacking in her kiss. Swallowing her gasp, he licked at her lips until they parted. His tongue moved inside, not rough, not intrusive, but demanding nonetheless. Demanding her response. Demanding her surrender.

Which she unhesitatingly gave. It was in her moan. In the way her hands moved from his hair to behind his neck, pulling him closer. In the way her body plastered itself to his.

In seconds, they were back on the couch, but instead of fighting him, her body was pliant and open, welcoming him and asking him for more.

He ripped his mouth away and rested his forehead on hers. "I've wanted to kiss you again, Mattie. I've dreamed of it."

She smiled and he lowered his head, needing to suck on her pretty lips more than he needed his next breath. She kissed him with the same hunger and desperation for about thirty seconds. Then she stiffened and froze. When she pulled back, he barely refrained from begging her to stay.

Sighing, Dom let go of her and sat up.

"Tony." She seemed to have trouble catching her breath, but managed to choke out, "He—he didn't do it, Dom. I know it. I know him."

He thought of the speculation about Joel. About his own certainty that Joel would never have had anything to do with Guapo or taking his own life. That same certainty was reflected in Mattie's eyes.

Slowly, he held out his hand. This time she took it. He

pulled until they were both standing. Brushing back her hair, he nodded. "Okay. I believe you."

"You do? Why now?"

"Because I know you, Mattie. If you believed Tony was guilty, you'd tell me. You'd still fight to keep him safe, but you wouldn't risk another person's safety, especially Jordan's."

Tears filled her eyes and she reached out and pulled him toward her, hugging him tight. "Thank you for believing me." Pulling away, she swiped at her tears. "But what do we do next?"

Using the pads of his thumbs, he swiped away a few errant drops of moisture she'd missed. "We check in with Linda and see if she's awake. You pick up Jordan. We try to find your brother. But first tell me about the burglary on Linda's apartment. I read the police report she filed, and she told officers that she'd been receiving harassing phone calls."

Mattie's eyes widened. "That's right. She even changed her number because they'd gotten so bad. She never said she'd received any more after that, but they could totally be related."

"So, besides Tony, was there anyone in her life—ex-boyfriends, any defendants she mentioned—that might have a reason to hurt her." He raised his hands when she glared at him. "You know what I meant."

"No one she's mentioned."

"Did she ever mention a man named Mark Guapo to you?"

"No. We rarely talk about specific cases. Why would she?"

"He was a defendant she prosecuted several months ago."

When she said nothing, he prodded, "So you've never heard the name before? At work?"

"Guapo." Her brows furrowed. "It sounds vaguely familiar, but—"

"Judge Butler was the sitting judge."

"When?"

"Two months ago last week."

"I was probably assigned to a different courtroom at that time."

"Why's that?"

"Jordan wanted to go on vacation for her birthday. I took some time off and another court reporter came in to cover me. When I returned, Judge Butler was right in the middle of a big case. It could have been that one. Why is this Guapo person so important?"

"He might not be, but I'm just trying to explore all the bases." He paced in front of her for several minutes before pausing to sit beside her. "Mattie, when Dusty attacked you in court, did you notice anything unusual?"

"Like what?"

"I don't know," he growled, rising again to continue pacing. "But he was on something when he attacked you, and yesterday I found out he'd died of an overdose in his cell. Dusty was a small-time druggie. Smuggling drugs into the jail isn't uncommon but it's not easy either. Someone was supplying him. He said it was in exchange for making some noise in court, but there's something else going on. Something that I think might be related to this Guapo defendant, and in turn possibly Linda. You got close to Dusty—"

"You think this Guapo character sent Dusty to hurt someone in the courtroom? Judge Butler? Linda?"

"I don't know."

She stared at him, frustration plainly etched into her features. "Give me a second." Rising, she moved to the sink, grabbed a glass, filled it with water, and took a sip. When she raised the glass in inquiry, he shook his head. Seconds, then minutes ticked by as she stared into her glass. Suddenly, she lifted her head. "His grip was off," she said excitedly.

"What do you mean, off?"

"He grabbed me, he scratched me, but it wasn't with a full

grip. It was more tenuous. You know, as if he was holding something in his hand he didn't want to let go. Maybe it was drugs?"

"Could be." But not likely. Dom thought about it some more. "It could have been anything. A piece of paper. A manufactured weapon. But if he was holding something when he came into that courtroom, he wasn't when he left. I searched him and cuffed him myself."

"What if he accidentally dropped it?"

Dom froze and turned to stare at her. "What if he dropped it on purpose?"

Chapter 14

Even though the last twenty had gone unanswered, Mattie knocked once more on Tony's apartment door. "Tony," she finally called out. "Tony, if you're home, please answer the door."

But he didn't.

Just like he hadn't answered his home or cell phone, and hadn't responded to any of the messages she'd left. Where was he?

She walked back to her car, which she'd picked up at the courthouse. Dom had been distracted when he'd dropped her off, obviously still thinking about the inmate who'd attacked her and why he'd wanted inside the courtroom. She'd been distracted, too. All she'd been able to think about was Tony and the hurt she'd put on his face. Slipping her hand in her pocket, she fingered the key that Tony had given her in case of an emergency.

Did Dominic's questions about Tony amount to an emergency? Normally, she would think so, but she also remembered the way Tony had looked at her before he'd left her house. Using her key under such circumstances didn't seem right. Not when he thought she believed Dom over him.

She hadn't heard from Dominic. Jordan was safe at school now, but where was Tony?

A thought occurred to her and she straightened. Maybe he'd gone to the hospital to see Linda.

She was just about to get in her car when a shiny red Camaro pulled up to the curb behind her. A young man who barely looked old enough to have his driver's license stepped out. As he swaggered toward her, however, the hardness and chill in his eyes made her realize he'd probably seen and experienced enough for four lifetimes.

He glanced at Tony's apartment building. "You here to see Tony?"

The way he spoke, half singsongy and half lewd insinuation, made her knees weak and her stomach heave. Obviously sensing her unease, he stepped closer, grinned, and raised a hand to stroke her hair.

She knocked it away. "Keep your hands to yourself," she hissed.

"Oooo. Feisty."

She moved around him to open her car door, but he slammed it shut, his features quickly shifting from lewd to threatening. Refusing to cower, she asked, "How do you know Tony?"

He circled her, sniffing exaggeratedly at her neck. "Tony and I are friends as well as business associates."

I'm in public, she thought. *He won't try anything here.* Lifting her chin defiantly, she said, "Tony's not using anymore, so why don't you just leave him alone."

"Why don't we go inside and see old Tony instead."

"He's not home."

With a sudden move, he jerked her against him, his hands

seeming to be everywhere at once. She struggled, trying to scream but unable to force any sound louder than a whimper out of her throat.

"Let go of me," she finally gasped.

Distantly, Mattie heard the sound of brakes squealing. Then a shout. "Sabon!"

The man jerked around, cursed, dropped Mattie, and ran. Mattie staggered and fell to the ground, catching herself on her still healing palms.

Dom lunged out of his truck. "You okay?" he shouted.

She nodded. Instinctively, she reached out for him, but just as she did so, he turned away and gave chase.

Sabon was fast. Really fast. And it was obvious he was familiar with the neighborhood. He took every corner without hesitation. Jumped every fence as if he'd been vaulting them for years.

Dom pushed himself to go faster, his arms and legs pumping hard. Satisfaction filled him as he gained on the man and prepared to grab him by the back of his black sweatshirt. The blare of a horn and the screech of brakes registered just as he caught sight of something huge in his periphery.

Dom swerved and threw himself to the side, landing on the asphalt with a jarring thud. He felt the air next to him vibrate as the silver Lexus's tires screeched to a halt just a few inches from his splayed legs. On his back and breathing hard, he saw the car's bumper roll into Sabon so that he momentarily flipped onto its hood. In a fluid motion, he rolled off and started running again, almost without breaking stride. Dom scrambled to his feet and skirted around the hood of the car, only to watch Sabon disappear.

He clenched his fists and slowly became aware of the pain radiating from his palms. Raising his hands, he saw they were scraped raw from where he'd caught himself on the ground. He glanced once more in the direction that Sabon had run, then pounded his fist on the Lexus's hood.

By the time he made it back to Mattie, she was leaning against her car and he was furious, only he wasn't sure at whom. Sabon for sure, for daring to put his hands on her. Him for letting it happen. And her for putting herself in danger in the first place. He strode up to her, not stopping until he'd hemmed her in with his arms.

They were both breathing hard.

"Did you meet him here?"

She shook her head. Closed and opened her mouth like a fish out of water.

He gripped her arms and shook her gently. "Did you, Mattie? Did you agree to meet him here?"

"I—I came to see Tony."

Dropping his hands, he stepped back. "Then that makes two of us."

"Who—who was that man?" she gasped out.

He studied her. The fear. The innocence.

Uncertainty overwhelmed him. When he'd left Mattie, he'd checked Judge Butler's courtroom and found a listening device right under the table where he'd pushed Dusty. That listening device was also a GPS tracker, the kind currently being tested by SWAT as a hostage negotiation tool. That meant the department could have a mole, most likely Frank Manelli. The only question was whether Manelli had given the bug to Dusty or Guapo voluntarily. And what role Tony played in it all.

When Mattie continued to stare at him, he struggled with how much to tell her. Normally, he'd opt for hiding as much as possible from her, but Tony was the key to solving this case, he was sure of it. And Mattie was his best chance of finding him.

* * *

Mattie stared at Dom, willing him to answer. Had that horrible man persuaded Tony to start up with drugs again? An involuntary whimper escaped her, one that Dom heard. He closed his eyes, released her, then stepped back.

"That was Michael Sabon—Mark Guapo's brother," he clarified. "The current leader of Guapo's crime organization, which specializes in drugs, stolen property and now firearm sales. I think Sabon is orchestrating Guapo's revenge against his defense attorney, Linda, and Judge Butler. Only he's not doing it alone. He's been getting help. And do you think it's just coincidence that he showed up at Tony's apartment?"

That man was Guapo's brother? "You're not really a courtroom bailiff, are you?" She should have realized it sooner, she thought, but his sudden appearance and Linda's attack had shaken her. Plus, he was a cop, so it had seemed perfectly natural for him to ask questions. What she hadn't realized until now was that he'd been the *only* cop asking them. All the questions he'd been asking about Tony, all the speculation he'd made about Judge Butler and this man named Guapo—they all pointed to him being a detective working a case. Which meant he'd been lying to her this whole time.

She saw the truth in his clenched jaw. In the hand he ran through his hair. And in the brief flash of guilt in his eyes.

"I'm a vice detective. Working as a bailiff was just a cover so I could get closer to Judge Butler and his staff."

Well, he'd certainly gotten closer to her, she thought bitterly, remembering their tussle on her couch. The feeling of betrayal came swift and hard.

Thank God she hadn't told him about Tony.

"Tell me why you originally thought Tony might have been the one to hurt Linda," he commanded softly.

Her head snapped up and she told herself to get it together. It was always his job that mattered most to him. In the end, it was all he cared about. "You used me. And you would have kept on using me to get information."

He shook his head. "It wasn't like that, Mattie, but I can't ignore the fact Sabon is trying to find your brother. If he's as innocent as you think he is, he's going to need all the help he can get. For once, trust me. Let me help you."

Her mouth and jaw tightened into mutinous lines that she knew echoed the mistrust in her eyes. "You want to ask me questions? You'll have to arrest me and bring me down to the station first. And I'm going to have an attorney with me when you do."

They stared at each other, neither one giving an inch.

"Fine," Dom finally said, his expression telling her this wasn't over. "But tell me, did you ever make it to the door to see if your brother is home?"

"I knocked. No one answered."

He glanced at the door. "I think I should go check for myself, don't you? After all, it is my *job*, as distasteful as that it is to you. Did you check whether the door was open? Do you have a key?"

She stiffened, giving herself away.

Dom sighed and held out his palm. "Why don't you give me the key and I'll check?"

"No."

"Will you stop being so stubborn for once? What if he's hurt, Mattie? How do you know Sabon wasn't returning after paying Tony a visit earlier?"

Her eyes widened. Automatically, she reached into her pocket and tried to dodge around him. He grabbed her arm and turned her around, his muscular arm wrapped around her waist.

"Stop it," he ordered in her ear. "I'm not letting you walk in there in a panic. Give me the key and I'll check on him. I promise."

"Both of us," she gasped. "I'll stay behind you, but we both have to go in. I'm not letting you walk into Tony's apartment without me."

Slowly, he released her and held out his hand again. After a brief hesitation, she placed the key in his palm.

"You stay behind me. If I tell you to run, you damn well run, do you understand?"

Curtly, she nodded. "Just don't tell me to run because you see Tony. I don't believe Tony will hurt me. I never will."

"Fine."

He walked to Tony's door with her right behind him, her hand automatically rising to rest on his back. He knocked loudly. "Tony, this is Dominic Jeffries. I'm with the Sacramento Police Department and I'm a friend of Mattie's. I need to ask you some questions."

Silence.

He knocked again. Announced himself even louder.

Nothing.

He looked at Mattie, who nodded her head. Placing the key in the lock, Dominic turned it and then opened the door. He motioned for her to wait, stepped inside the apartment, and called, "Tony?"

Even though she no longer touched him, she saw the muscles in his back and shoulders bunch. But instead of stepping farther inside, he stepped back, shut the door, and turned back toward her, his face grim.

"Let's go," he commanded. He took her arm and urged her down the path toward her car.

She pulled back. "You're not going in?"

"Come with me. Now, Mattie." His voice was clipped. His eyes intense.

She tilted her head and backed away from him. "You saw something, didn't you?"

His expression hardened and he came after her. "Mattie—Mattie, no!"

She lunged toward the door and threw it open. Instantly, Dominic's fingers wrapped around her arm and he pulled her outside, but not before she saw the body.

"Damn you, Mattie."

Despite his grip on her arm, Mattie's knees gave out and she immediately slumped to the ground. Bright dots flashed in front of her eyes and she heard Dom's voice from a great distance, asking her if she was okay.

Why was he asking her if she was okay? she thought hysterically. She was fine.

The same couldn't be said for Judge Butler.

Chapter 15

Mattie tried to disappear into her seat as Dominic drove her car. After dealing with the police officers who'd arrived in response to his 911 call, he'd refused to let her drive home herself and she'd refused to leave her only method of transportation at Tony's. Every few minutes, she felt his gaze on her, but she refused to acknowledge him until he took an exit towards downtown. She sat up. "Where are you—we need to pick up Jordan!"

"I called Jordan's school. She's fine. I've arranged for a plainclothes officer to pick her up and take her to her grandparents' house."

"What? How dare you!" Enraged, she grabbed the wheel, gasping when he pushed her away and pulled to the side of the road. As soon as he put the car in Park, she was on him, pounding him with her fists, slapping at his face. "I want my daughter. I need to go to her now!" she screamed.

"Stop, Mattie." With sickening ease, he gripped her wrists

and held her away from him. "Stop and think. We need to keep her safe and that's the best way to do it."

Her breath caught at his words. "Let me go."

Slowly, he did. Sitting as far from him as she could, she rubbed her wrists, noting the way his gaze guiltily followed her movements. "You think someone would go after her at school?"

"We have no reason to think that, but I'm not taking any chances. Not with our daughter."

The last two words flowed easily off his tongue. So easily, in fact, Mattie stiffened. "But you still think she'll be safe at John's parents'?"

"I've arranged for a patrol officer to stay with them. It was tough getting the man hours approved, but when I told the lieutenant about Judge Butler—" He faced the windshield and slammed a fist against the steering wheel before glancing at her again. "Taking her to her grandparents' house is the best bet."

"But you're afraid whoever hurt Linda, whoever killed Judge Butler, is going to come after me next. That's why I can't stay with Jordan."

He pressed his lips together. "I want to protect you both, Mattie."

"And what do I do in the meantime?"

"You keep yourself safe until you can go to her. I'm not going to let what happened to Linda or Judge Butler happen to you."

Judge Butler. At the sound of his name, she blinked rapidly, trying to stop the sudden flow of tears that gathered in her eyes. Cursing, Dom reached for her once more. She shook her head. Tried to hold herself stiff against him. But the instant Dom pulled her into his chest, she couldn't contain her grief any longer. Like a decrepit building, already unsteady and brought down by a blast of dynamite, she crumbled.

Sobs tore through her and her body heaved with her efforts to regain control.

"It's going to be okay." Dom stroked her hair and she grasped at his shirt, not understanding how her life had turned upside down so quickly.

"He's dead," she gasped out. "And why? Because he sentenced a horrible man to prison? And what about Tony? What if he's hurt, too?"

"I have men looking for him now. They'll bring him in."

It was the way he said it that made her lean back. "He didn't do it, Dom."

He didn't flinch from her gaze, but his eyes didn't soften either. "Right now, we just need to make sure you and Jordan are safe. Okay?"

She nodded. After squeezing her hand once, he pulled back on the road.

They continued to drive in silence until Dom said, "It's not just a job for me, you know."

"What?"

"This assignment," he clarified, still facing forward, his fingers gripping the steering wheel so hard his knuckles whitened. "I didn't like lying to you. I don't like lying in general. But undercover work exists for a reason. And this isn't just another assignment for me. I have a vested interest in the parties involved." He looked at her now, his gaze steady. "You. Jordan. Your brother. Joel. But in the end, you're what's at stake. And I'm sorry, but if it takes lying to keep you safe and keep a dangerous man in jail, I'll do it every time."

He faced forward again, leaving Mattie to stare at his profile, speechless. Despite his stark expression, she'd heard the emotion behind his words, as well as the resolve. Only what could she say in return? Even if he hadn't lied to her, nothing had changed. Her sneering thoughts about his "super cop" mentality aside, she'd never doubted his ultimate goal as a cop was an honorable one. But it was still the goal that seemed to keep them apart. "Who's Joel?"

"My ex-partner."

"You said he was another reason this assignment is so important to you. Is Guapo after him, too?"

"Guapo killed him," he said starkly. "Although some think he was dirty. That he killed himself."

The car stopped and she realized they were in front of her house. He didn't move, just continued to stare out the window. Moving slowly, she inched closer, reached out, and turned his face toward her. Her breath hitched.

His eyes were clouded over with pain.

"But you don't believe that?"

Instead of answering, he pulled the door open, stepping out of the car so her hand fell away. Just like that, it was as if he'd flipped a switch, taking the man away from her and leaving only the cop. "I'm going to check inside. Wait here."

He was back within minutes. "It's all clear. Come inside."

She followed him and stepped inside her house, feeling like she was dragging the world's ugliness in with her. She turned toward Dom, who was watching her closely. "How can you stand it? How can you deal with this day in and day out?"

He frowned. "Somebody has to do it. And I can handle it better than most."

Could he? she wondered for the first time. Or did he just think he had to for some reason? "Don't you want more than that?"

She knew they were both thinking of Jordan at that moment.

"Wanting more doesn't enter the equation. I do what has to be done. And right now, Mattie, I need you to answer some questions for me."

"How about you answer a question for me first?"

Surprise flickered across his face, but he nodded.

"Would you have stayed with me, if you'd known about Jordan?"

He didn't hesitate. "Yes."

"Would you have been a cop?"

This answer came more slowly. "Probably not."

"Would you have resented me?"

He didn't answer for several minutes. Finally, he sighed and raked both hands through his hair. "I'd like to think not, but can I say for sure? No. Being a cop is who I am. Sometimes it feels like it's all I am. But no matter what, I'd have taken care of you, if you'd have let me. I know that much."

She swallowed hard, his answer sinking into her bones. She believed him. In fact, she'd never really doubted otherwise. Had it been wrong for her to deprive Jordan of her father because she'd selfishly wanted Dom to stay with her because of love and not obligation?

Walking to one of the living room bookcases, she pretended to straighten a picture frame. She stared at the picture of John and Jordan dressed as the Scarecrow and Dorothy for their last Halloween together. There was joy on their faces, but it had all been an illusion in the end. Ultimately, she and Jordan only had each other. Not even Tony was a sure thing.

Feeling utterly alone in that moment, she turned back to Dom, who was now staring at the floor, looking even more alone than she felt. His defeated posture reminded her that while she'd deprived Jordan of a father, she'd also deprived him of a daughter. Someone to give him hope when things were at their lowest.

"Why do people think Joel killed himself?" she asked.

His head jerked up. A slight flush colored his cheekbones, his calm façade cracking slightly. "Because that's what the evidence suggests. Even Tawny, his wife… I saw the doubt in her eyes at the funeral. After Joel gave up everything for her, how could she—" His voice faltered and he glanced around the room, almost if he was looking for a way to escape. A place to hide before he let her get another rare glimpse of the man inside the cop.

She walked closer to him, refusing to let him hide. "Sometimes it's hard for people to have that much faith in someone else. And fleeting doubt isn't the same as betrayal." She said it pointedly, taking his face in her hands when he wouldn't look at her. "It's not, Dominic."

He tried to pull away, but she followed him, taking his hands.

"I'm not saying I—" he began.

"I know. But just in case, you need to remember what you do for a living. You are a cop. Like you said, your job is to cover every base. I understand now. I understand why you have to ask questions about Tony. Even me. And if you've had to ask questions about Joel, that's okay, too. That's how you survive. It's how you do your job."

He twisted his hands until he softly gripped her wrists, rubbing his thumbs against her pulse points, making her skin heat from the outside in. "He was my best friend—"

"And you loved him. You miss him."

Not thinking of anything but wanting to comfort him, she rose on tiptoe and hugged him.

Dom didn't return Mattie's embrace.

Thoughts of Joel and Judge Butler and Mattie and Jordan were swirling in his head with enough force to make him dizzy. She clearly wanted him to release his tight grip on his emotions, and though it was slipping, he desperately held on to what was left. Being a cop meant having to suppress any emotion that would get in the way of the job. It meant having to view the evidence objectively and, just as she'd said, consider things you didn't want to, even about people you loved.

Although he'd initially denied it, part of him had eventually questioned whether Joel had killed himself. As a cop, he'd had to, but the guilt still weighed heavily on him. She'd obviously seen that somehow.

Despite his stiffness, she didn't back away. She simply held him and he let her. After several minutes, he realized the pain in his gut was gone. He could breathe a little easier. It was there—that same sense of "rightness," of ease, that his body always felt when he was with Mattie.

It telegraphed loud and clear how much he needed her.

His heart pumped hard, shoving blood into his extremities. Making his fingers tingle. Making his skin heat.

Making him realize how lost he'd been without her and how lost he'd be if he let her walk away from him again. This time, with his daughter.

Instinctively, he rejected the very idea of letting his daughter go. But he'd been afraid of disappointing Mattie if he stayed with her. How much more would he disappoint a little girl?

Back away. Back away now.

But even as he braced himself to step back from Mattie, his body had other ideas.

He wrapped his arms around her, and buried his face in the curve between her neck and shoulder. Mattie stiffened at first, then slowly relaxed against him. He shuddered as her warmth and fragrance wrapped around him, gentle and comforting.

She raised her hands to his shoulders, then to his skull, petting him in slow, easy circles. "It's okay," she murmured. Her hands caressed his face and he pulled back to look at her. She kissed his forehead, offering him solace in a way he'd never experienced before.

In a way he might never again.

He kissed her, a light touch of his lips on hers, gone almost before it started. Then he did it again, gracing her jawline with one kiss after another. She shivered when he kissed the soft skin behind her ear.

"Dominic?"

"Shhh," he said. "Not yet. Just let me—" He took her mouth again, this time with a fierce, almost desperate melding of lips and teeth and tongue. They'd been together only a few months before their split, and their reunion had covered mere days, but it felt like he'd wanted her forever. He'd never wanted anyone the way he wanted Mattie.

He tilted his head and took her from a different angle, deepening the kiss. His hands snaked under her shirt, making her jerk when his cool skin pressed against her warmth. She moaned and pulled him closer, her hands ripping at the buttons of his shirt, encouraging him to take more.

Forcing himself to leave her mouth just long enough to pull her shirt over her head, he immediately latched back on only to pull down her pants and underwear. She kicked them out of the way and undid his jeans, inserting a hand and cupping him until he gritted his teeth at the pleasure. Grabbing her wrist, he pulled her hand away, lifted her up until her legs wound around his waist, and speed walked into the bedroom.

Once there, he laid her on the bed and took in her splayed thighs and the treasure between them. Slowly, softly, he touched her. She was wet, so wet, and he instantly froze, eyes closed, trying to absorb every hint of sensation. Her head fell back, as did his own.

Their breathing synchronized, ragged and deep. He buried his face in her neck and parted her with his fingers, trying to reach into the very heart of her.

"Dominic," she moaned, her voice rising just as she started to contract around his fingers, milking him with a firm, rhythmic squeeze of velvet and silk.

"So good," he gasped. "You feel so good." He pulled

himself up to look at her, but her eyes were closed. "Look at me," he grated, his voice sounding foreign to his own ears. Gravelly. Primitive. All pretenses shattered.

She did, but her eyes were dazed. "Let me touch you," she whispered, trying to pull away from him.

He shook his head. "Bend your knees," he encouraged. "Open yourself to me. All of you."

She hesitated then complied, bending her knees, exposing herself, putting herself in his care. Gently, he pulled her toward him at the same time he scooped each leg onto one arm, and pressed her out and open until she was completely exposed to him. He gripped her wrists again and poised himself at her entrance.

"This is what I want. I want you to look into my eyes and know how desperate I am for you. That there's nothing you can do, nothing you can say, that would stop me from wanting this." He teasingly slipped just the tip of himself into her, shaking at the effort of holding back. "Tell me you want me."

She struggled against his grip, trying to envelop more of him inside her.

"Tell me you want me. Tell me I'm all you've ever wanted. Me over you. Me inside you. Even if it's just for the moment."

"You know I—"

"Tell me, Mattie. Please."

She froze and stared into his eyes. He let her see it all. His yearning. His desperation.

Her breath caught and she nodded. "I want you. Over me. Inside of me. You're—" She swallowed hard and her eyes filled with tears. "You're all I've ever wanted."

She hadn't even finished the sentence before he was inside her. He let go of her wrists, wrapped himself around her, and thrust deep. He gritted his teeth at the way her short nails bit through the fabric of his shirt. Within minutes, she came, but he still didn't let himself go. He pulled back and tilted her chin up so he could look into her beautiful eyes.

"I want you to remember this moment. Remember how much you want me. How much you need this."

She nodded, but it wasn't enough for him.

He groaned as he felt himself getting close. "Promise me," he gasped out. "Promise me you won't for—" Suddenly, he couldn't speak. The tremors overtook him, dragging a hoarse, animalistic shout from the depths of his soul. "Mattie!"

His body jerked in a series of fading tremors. When it was over, he could barely move. She rubbed his back, caressing him with firm, steady strokes. "I promise," she whispered. "I promise."

She said it again. And again. Until all he could do was tighten his arms around her and welcome sleep.

She woke sometime during the night to find him staring at her, trailing his fingers across her body the way he'd done so many times in the past. She stretched languidly, unashamed of her nudity, relishing the way his eyes darkened and his breathing sped up. The air felt heavy, her skin warm. If she didn't know better, she'd think she was dreaming about him again.

She didn't realize she'd spoken her thoughts until he said, "This is no dream." He grinned and bent to kiss her, flicking his tongue lightly against her lips until she moaned. Instead of penetrating her deeper, he pulled back. "But if it was," he teased, "and you could control it, what would you have us do?"

Murmuring in protest, she rose up and tried to capture his mouth, but he pulled just out of reach. "Come on, Mattie. Tell me one of your fantasies. Something you've never done, never told anyone, but always wanted to try."

She stared up at him, feeling as if she was in a daze. Her

inhibitions seemed to have melted away and she wondered if someone had injected her with honey. She felt all warm and tingly. Soft. Womanly.

Edible.

Savor-able.

The word echoed in her mind, causing her to speak without thinking. "Handcuffs," she whispered.

His eyes narrowed just before he buried his face in the crook of her neck. There, he sprinkled several kisses across her skin before biting her with a sharp nip that made her moan. Then, before she knew it, he was gone and pulling on his jeans. She shoved herself up on her elbows. "What—?"

"Don't move," he ordered.

He exited the bedroom, and she heard the front door open and close. He was back inside in under a minute. He lifted his hand, showing her the cuffs dangling from his fingers. She immediately snickered and held out her hands. Dom tossed them to her.

He placed a key on the night table, then, with his jeans still on, sat beside her. "Now, where were we?"

She sighed when he took her mouth, this time giving her the deep, wet kiss she was longing for. Then a thought occurred to her and she pulled away. "Wait a minute," she breathed with a hand to his chest. "Have you ever—?"

He shook his head. "I've never used handcuffs with a woman. I swear."

Well, at least that was something.

He tilted his head as he looked at her. "If you've changed your mind about being tied up, we can forget about the cuffs and just get to the good part, you know." He reached out to take the cuffs from her and she quickly moved away, holding them out of his reach.

She wagged a finger at him. "Uh-uh-uh. Who said anything about me being tied up? You asked me about my fantasy and yes, handcuffs are involved. But in my fantasy, I'm not the one wearing them."

He leaned back against one of the bedposts. "Is that a fact?"

"That's right. Does that scare you?"

"Not at all." Before she could express her skepticism, he lowered his hand to his jeans then paused. With a questioning look, he asked, "I'm assuming you want me naked?"

"Uh. Sure," she said, unable to tear her gaze from the light dusting of hair that arrowed into his jeans. Unable to believe he was willing to accommodate her without a fight.

"You sure? Because if you had something else in mind…"

"No." The word came out a little faint, so she cleared her throat and spoke louder. "Naked is good."

"Great." Methodically, he stripped off his jeans. When he was finished, he stood in front of her, completely at ease with his nudity. Staring at him, her mouth went dry and her knees trembled.

Despite how wonderful making love with him had been, she hadn't had the opportunity to simply look at him or to take her time touching him. She wanted to do both. To reacquaint herself with his body. As much as she wanted. For as long as she wanted.

She suddenly understood what he was giving her. Complete and total access. Complete control. And complete accountability. This wasn't about being swept away by passion, but grabbing it by the throat with full knowledge of who and what Dom was.

"Should I lie down?"

Biting her lip, she nodded, unsure of her ability to speak. He immediately lay down on the bed and stretched his arms above his head. "You need help with the cuffs?"

"I think I can do it." She stepped beside him, amazed at how unconcerned he appeared. Not unaffected—he was long and hard, spearing out from his belly like a warrior eager for battle—but completely comfortable with putting himself, literally, in her hands. Unable to help herself, she reached out and trailed her fingers over him.

He clenched his fists and hissed, but otherwise didn't move.

Doubt suddenly swept through her. Once he was tied down, it was all up to her. What if she choked? What if he got so bored he fell asleep? As ridiculous as her thoughts were, they still had her hesitating. "You know, I'm not sure—"

"Here. I'll show you how they work." Gently, he took the cuffs from her, slipped his left wrist in one, snapped it closed, and then hooked it on the bedpost. He held out the other cuff. "Now you do the other one."

Silently, she stared at the cuff. "Okay." Taking if from him, she slipped it on his right wrist and tightened it. When she moved to connect the chain to the bedpost, however, he said, "Wait."

She froze.

"Come here." The command came out hoarse, as if he was having trouble breathing.

She'd lost her ability to breathe a long time ago. "Why?"

"Because before you tie me down, I need to do something."

She leaned slightly toward him.

"Closer," he whispered.

She leaned down even farther, until her long hair brushed against his face. He brought his hand toward her and she expected him to cup her breast or the hot spot between her legs. She actually moaned in anticipation. Instead, he tucked her hair behind her ear and then rubbed the back of his fingers against her cheek. Startled, she nuzzled into his touch like a cat begging to be petted, but kept her gaze glued to his. He just stared at her for several seconds, a mysterious smile on his lips, and then he dropped his hand. "Okay, I'm ready."

She blinked. "That was it?"

"Yeah." The single word was fraught with contentment. As if he could die at that moment with no regrets.

Feeling stronger and more powerful than she ever had, she attached the restraint to the other bedpost. "How's that?"

He tugged on both wrists, then grinned. "I'm at your mercy. Do your worst."

"Are you kidding?" she asked. She climbed up the foot of the bed, forcing him to spread his legs in order to make room for her. She prowled toward him on all fours, not stopping until she straddled his waist. He hissed and arched as she brushed against his erection, and she closed her eyes at the feel of him sliding against her backside. With a teasing smile, she planted a hand on either side of his head, bending over him so that her nipples just hovered over his chest. She pressed a light kiss on his shoulder, then rose to stare into his dazed eyes. "I have a job to do and doing my worst isn't in the plan. Not when I can do my best."

Dom was dying of pleasure. Sweat covered his body and his skin felt like it was on fire. Her slightest touch caused pleasure to pool in his shaft, making him so hard it actually hurt. He lost track of time and measured its passage by how desperately he urged her to touch him.

First, he asked her to take him in her mouth.

Then, he told her to wrap her fingers around him.

Soon, he was commanding her to finish it.

She ignored him, rubbing her nipples across his chest, trailing kisses up one thigh and down the other, licking his nipples with slow, languid strokes of her tongue and then gently biting them. His hips were in perpetual motion, searching for release even as he marveled at her power over him. He'd even started to beg, but no matter what he said or did, she ignored the part of him that longed most for her attention.

"Baby, I can't take much more," he moaned. "I need you. Please."

She'd returned to her favorite position, straddling his waist as she rubbed her breasts against him and kissed his nipples. When she didn't respond to his plea, he pulled at the restraints on his wrists, frantic to get inside her. She raised herself up on her knees, cupped her breasts, and stared down at him with the most beautiful expression he'd ever seen.

He was in awe. Mattie was charged up and taking no prisoners. For the moment, everything else in the world was forgotten and he was determined to make it last. He gritted his teeth and rode it out, each second seeming to stretch into days. At one point, he actually entered a trancelike state, his mind slightly detached from the sensations tormenting his body. Then she did something that almost sent him hurtling over the edge.

Lifting her head, she stared down at him, her face flushed, her eyes dilated, but instead of obeying him, she smiled wickedly, lifted the hand she'd been using to touch herself, and slipped her fingers into his mouth.

He snapped. "Unlock me, Mattie."

Her eyes widened at the guttural, naked command in his voice. Visibly trembling, she took the key and fumbled with the cuffs until finally he was free. He grabbed hold of her hips and plunged into her.

She moaned, a long, almost tormented sound that shivered over him until he knew he couldn't hold back any longer. When she screamed out her pleasure, he let himself go, coming in violent pulses, coming harder than he'd ever come before.

He thought he must have passed out. When his brain kicked in, he turned his head and looked at her. She was out cold. He tried to lift his hand so that he could pull the blanket over her, only he couldn't. He felt as weak as a newborn baby and just as vulnerable.

But even though he was weak, his resolve was strong. She destroyed him. And no matter what it took, he was going to make her his again. In return, he would be hers.

Unfortunately, he still had to travel the road from here to there.

With a sigh, he closed his eyes and acknowledged the road was going to be damn difficult. Because before he could give himself fully to Mattie, he needed to be the one person she hated most.

He needed to be the cop.

Her body ached, but in a pleasant way, as if her muscles had been kneaded and worked and wrung out after a particularly grueling day at work. Heat surrounded her, pulling her more deeply towards sleep even as it evaporated the air around her, making it difficult to breathe.

Mattie tried turning on her side, but something heavy pinned her down. Her eyelids twitched as the smell of Dom and sex and her own body teased her senses. She burrowed closer to the source of heat at her side, ready to surrender to the dark once more.

She felt something against her cheek and flinched. "Mattie. Mattie, wake up. Come on, baby."

She recognized Dom's voice instantly.

"Dominic," she whispered, trying to pry open her eyelids. When she finally succeeded, his face swam in front of her and then came into focus. He smiled at her and she felt her heart lurch.

"Hi," he said softly, pushing her hair away from her face with such tenderness that she automatically turned her face to kiss his hand. His breath hissed as he inhaled. She looked around.

Memories registered one after the other.

His confession about his friend.

The way he'd wrapped himself around her, as if she was the only thing on earth he needed.

His fierce passion and his unwavering determination to make her admit she wanted him.

The ways they'd made love. Again and again. No inhibitions. Every fantasy fulfilled.

As he stared at her, his gaze hot and intense, she suddenly realized that while she was completely naked, he was not. The contrast between her wanton nudity and his obvious control made her cringe.

She struggled to a sitting position even as she grabbed a sheet to cover herself. His eyes followed the movement, darkening when they skimmed across her body, but then shuttering.

"We got a little sidetracked."

Flummoxed, Mattie stared at him. Guilt flooded her. For the time she was in his arms, she'd forgotten her fear and grief. She'd forgotten about Tony and Judge Butler. For a time, she'd even forgotten about Jordan.

And although he'd given her a taste of pleasure, how much harder would it be to live without it now?

Silence grew heavy between them.

"Mattie, we need to talk about Tony."

Gone was the needy lover who'd made her body weep with pleasure. In his place was the cop with a mission. And she was just another means for him to gather evidence for his case.

She swallowed hard and took a deep breath, talking as she quickly put her clothes back on. "He got into drugs after our parents died. It started out small, but kept getting progressively worse."

"He tried rehab?"

"Repeatedly. He'd always slip up. Eventually, he started to get angrier. Do things I never would have thought he would."

"Did he ever hurt you?"

"Not physically. But he would say things. Steal things. It was really hard for a long time."

"Then what happened?"

"Linda happened. He loved her, but he blew it. I thought losing her had finally made him turn a corner."

"I think you're right. I think he decided to give up the drug life in a major way."

Wide-eyed she stared at him. "What do you mean?"

"I think Tony wanted to go straight and wanted to help get rid of his supplier, despite the risk. What better way to prove his resolve to Linda?"

"And his supplier was Guapo? Sabon?"

"That's what I'm thinking. I think Tony called the station and got in touch with an officer there named Frank Manelli. Manelli applied for a warrant to search Guapo's premises. To get it, he filed an affidavit, citing information from a confidential informant. Guess which judge authorized it?"

"Judge Butler?"

"Judge Butler."

"Okay, so why can't we call this Officer Manelli and find out if Tony is the one who talked to him?"

"Because Manelli's been missing. Ever since Joel was murdered. We don't know if it's because Guapo took him down, as one of the major officers who searched the premises, or if he's now working for Guapo."

"But if Manelli's working for Guapo, and he knows Tony is the confidential informant, that means Tony's life is in danger, too. That's what you've been trying to tell me."

"I'm telling you it's a possibility. The bug I found in the courtroom is very high-tech stuff. If Dusty planted the bug in the courtroom, it's very possible he got it from the officer who arrested him—Manelli."

Mattie gripped his arm. "What are you going to do?"

"I need to find Tony. Fast. He'll need protection if Guapo or Sabon really suspect him. If they don't, he still might be able to give us an advantage in tracking down the person who hurt Linda."

"What do you mean?"

"Just that they know him. And they trusted him once. If they don't suspect that he snitched them out…"

As his words trailed off, Mattie slowly rose. "Then what?"

"Mattie—" He reached out to her, but she wouldn't let him touch her.

"You'd use him again? Even though he's already in danger from having helped the police once?"

"We're getting ahead of ourselves, Mattie. We don't know if that's the case."

"But what if it is? What if Tony does have an in with Sabon? With Guapo? What then?"

"He could save lives, Mattie. What about Linda? If there had been a way to stop that, don't you think he would have wanted to?"

"Don't you dare use her to support your argument. That's unfair."

"Why? Because you care about both of them?"

"Because you're telling me that you would willingly use my brother to help you with a case. If he helped the police once, it was because he wanted out of that world. And you'd have him go back in?"

"I'd be there, too, Mattie. Undercover operations are some of the most well thought out and strategically planned. We just don't run in without making sure everything's covered. We don't just set up a sting and go in and arrest people. We make sure our operatives aren't compromised."

"Tony is not an operative. He's a waiter. He's a recovering drug addict."

"I'm sorry," he said starkly, his expression radiating regret. "I don't know what to say."

"Say that you won't do it. Say that if you have a choice between choosing to use my brother—use me—to help with a case or not, that you'd choose not to."

His eyes narrowed with a combination of anger and frustration. "Do you think I want to use him? Do you think I want to use anyone? I do what I need to in order to get the job done. But sometimes I need help. Sometimes, everyday people need to have the courage to stand with the cops. And in this case, I owe it to Joel and his wife to find out what happened to him. Having someone on the inside could help me do that."

"So you're saying no? You won't leave him out of it?"

"If I thought I needed him, Mattie, it would be his choice. I wouldn't force him to do anything he didn't want to do."

She smiled sadly. "That's not good enough. Goodbye, Dominic."

"Don't do this, Mattie. You're asking me to give up who I am, to give up the opportunity to get a very dangerous man off the streets. To possibly prevent more deaths, if not from Sabon directly, then from the drugs he deals."

"What about Jordan?" she asked bitterly. "Would you use her to obtain your precious justice?" Hurt flashed briefly on his face, but Mattie was too angry to accept it for what it was.

"Is that what you really think? That I would willingly use a child? *My* child?"

She said nothing, and his face closed up. He grabbed his jacket and put it on with jerky movements. "I'm telling you the only person you can trust right now is me. Not Tony. And not even yourself. If he contacts you, call me first. I'm his best protection."

"Don't pretend you care about his safety," she scoffed.

"I did my job well, didn't I? It's not just that you don't trust me. You really hate me, Mattie, don't you?"

Her mouth moved to answer, but she couldn't force any words out. His mouth twisted bitterly.

"It's okay. You don't have to answer that. I hear your answer loud and clear."

Chapter 16

On the drive to the station, Dom tried not to think about the hurt and betrayal on Mattie's face. He also tried not to remember the sweet feel and smell of her in his arms; chances were he'd never experience it again, so why torture himself?

Anger that hadn't quite cooled flamed yet again inside him. He'd known she'd be upset when he started asking questions again, but she'd actually had the gall to suggest he'd willingly put his own daughter in danger. All because he couldn't lie and promise to keep Tony completely out of the investigation. What was wrong with maneuvering circumstances to get the information needed for the greater good? If Tony was willing, why shouldn't they take advantage of that? He was a grown man, despite what Mattie seemed to think, and it wasn't as if Dom would force him into it.

Would he? The question pricked his conscience, compelling him to answer honestly. Force, maybe not. But he'd used strong persuasion in the past, hadn't he? Wouldn't he have brought up Tony's drug addiction to get him to help? Told him that he needed to do it to protect those he loved? To get justice for Judge Butler and Linda? To protect Mattie and their daughter?

And what did that say about him? Was that carrying things too far?

Because it would certainly insure he would never see Mattie again.

That thought made the slow burn in his stomach suddenly explode. He grimaced and rubbed his side. It took more than a few deep breaths this time to make the pain disappear. When it did, he stared at the building in front of him.

This isn't about me, he reminded himself. *It's not even about Mattie. It's greater than that.* Tony was an adult who could make his own decisions. So Dom would do what he needed to do, just like always.

Slamming out of his truck, he strode into the station, then the back room where the detectives worked. Cam was pouring himself a cup of coffee. His eyes were shadowed, his jaw covered in the beginnings of a five-o'clock shadow. For Cam, the scruffiness was a surefire sign that Grace Manelli's rejection was weighing heavily on him.

"Cam, I'm looking for Lewis. I want him to track down a witness for me. One that might be related to the warrant Frank wrote up in the Guapo case."

"Lewis is off. Anything I can help with?"

"I'm trying to track down a guy by the name of Tony Cooper. I have reason to believe he may have information on the Guapo case."

"What kind of information?"

"I'm not sure yet, but I think he might have been the CI who talked to Frank."

"And you can't look for him, why?"

"I'm looking for him, too. I just want to cover more

ground. If I'm right, then this guy's life is in danger. I need him protected and fast."

"Why? So you can get more info on Guapo?"

"No. Because he's Mattie Nolan's brother."

Mattie's phone had been ringing off and on ever since Dominic had left. Each time, the caller ID told her that the caller wasn't Tony, the hospital, or her in-laws, so she let it ring, wanting to shut out the world for just a while until she could figure out what she was going to do.

Dominic's blatant honesty about his willingness to use Tony had angered her, but after replaying their argument over and over again, she had to admit she hadn't exactly been fair. She'd let her fear of the intimacy they'd just shared drive her when he'd shown her time and again his main motivation was fairness and justice. He wouldn't understand Tony's weakness for drugs in the first place, and would probably see his willingness to help the police as some kind of penance owed.

It wasn't the same, not to him, as using her or Jordan.

Still, it made no difference. Tony was her brother and she wouldn't allow him to risk himself that way, which meant she and Dominic were still at opposite ends of the spectrum. He'd risk himself and others for justice—she wasn't willing to do either. But that didn't mean she hated him, and the vile things she'd said to him had been wrong.

When her phone rang, she expected it to be another unknown caller. Instead, the display blinked with Tony's cell phone number. "Tony! Where are you? I've been looking everywhere—"

"Linda." His voice cracked and Mattie cringed at the grief enveloping the sound. "I needed to see her, but there's a police officer posted outside. I'm afraid that cop of yours will have me arrested if I try to see her."

When had Dominic become "her" cop? Oddly, despite their fight, the moniker felt right.

"He thinks I want to hurt her," Tony whispered. "Just like you do."

She'd known her brother all her life. The hurt and grief in his voice wasn't an act. "No, Tony. I never said I believed that."

"I saw it in your eyes, Mattie."

"You're wrong," she insisted, remembering what she'd told Dom. Working through a scenario or questioning what the evidence appeared to be wasn't the same as believing Tony had hurt Linda. Deep down, she'd always believed in Tony's innocence. That's why she'd been so reluctant to talk to Dom about him. Doing so had felt too much like conceding Tony's guilt. "Whatever you saw, you're wrong, Tony. I know you love Linda. That you'd never hurt her like that. I know you'd never hurt Judge Butler, either."

Silence filled the line and she wondered if he'd hung up.

"Judge Butler?" Tony's voice was stronger now. "What are you talking about?"

"He was—he was at your apartment, Tony. I used the key you gave me and when I went inside, he was there. He was dead. You haven't been back there?"

"No! I've been staying with a friend. This is the first time I've come outside."

"Tony, when I went to your apartment, a man named Michael Sabon was there. Do you think he killed Judge Butler?"

His hiss was audible over the phone line. "Did he talk to you? Did he hurt you, Mattie?"

"He grabbed me, but—"

"No! Damn it, no! I'm going to kill him, I swear."

"So, you do know him?" She couldn't help the slight accusation infused in the statement.

"He used to be my supplier. He's been trying to get me back in, but I've told him no, over and over again."

"Is he the one who called you on your cell phone when you were at my house?"

"Yes. I—I don't want to piss him off. There're things you don't know—"

"You mean that you're the informant that gave the police information on Guapo?"

"You know?"

"Dom figured it out. He thought Guapo would make an attempt on Judge Butler. And then when Linda—"

"Mattie, listen to me," Tony urged. "If the cop knows, then he might be the one working for Guapo. That man has spies everywhere. He's going to come after me, Mattie, and then he'll come after you. You need to leave—"

She grabbed her purse and rifled through it for her keys. There was no way she thought Dom was working with Guapo. "Stay where you are. I'm coming to get you. Will you wait for me there?"

"Where's Jordan?"

This time she didn't even hesitate to tell him. "She's with John's parents. Safe. I want you safe, too."

She held her breath in the silence that followed. Finally, Tony said, "I'll wait for you, Mattie, but then we're all getting out of here."

"We'll talk it about it when I see you. Just wait for me."

Mattie hung up the phone and stared at the receiver. Dom's voice haunted her. "If he contacts you, call me first. I'm his best protection." He hadn't said those words lightly, or just to scare her. But although she trusted him, Tony didn't. So she'd pick up Tony first and together they'd discuss their options.

She owed her brother that chance.

.Before she could change her mind, she opened the door. She froze when she saw the man standing there.

"We found Frank Manelli."

Dom's head snapped up at the lieutenant's voice. He'd been out on the street, driving around searching for Tony— at his apartment, at the restaurant he worked at, even going door to door to see if any of his neighbors had seen him— and had only come into the station to see if Cam was back. Upon hearing Frank's name, a rush of hope filled him. Frank Manelli was the one person who might be able to provide the information Dom needed to help Mattie's brother. When his gaze found the lieutenant, however, hope dissolved. From the look on the other man's face, Dom knew there was no chance Frank was going to be providing anything to anyone.

"Was there evidence that Guapo's killed him?"

"No." The lieutenant's face was pale, his eyes bloodshot. "Of course that's possible, hell, it's the most likely explanation, but not even Guapo's men have done anything quite like this. He was tortured, Dom."

"Where was he found?"

"In an old meth lab near Franklin Blvd. By the looks of things, he was there for a long time. The coroner placed time of death sometime yesterday. Grace is beside herself."

"My God." Despite his resolve, Dom's control slipped. The fact that Frank had been tortured, and that they hadn't been able to find him for so long, meant they were dealing with someone smart. Powerful. Without conscience.

"This was personal, Dom. A cop signing a warrant doesn't generate that kind of violence. Who could have hated Manelli that much?"

"I don't—" The words stalled in Dom's throat.

Frank's wife, Grace, beside herself with grief.

Frank taken by someone smart and powerful.

Why not the man that loved Frank's wife?

The man he'd sent after Mattie's brother.

Cam.

"No," Dom breathed.

After the fight with Mattie, he'd just wanted to cover twice as much ground. Wanted to get Tony someplace safe so he could prove to her that he had everyone's interests in mind, not just his own. While he'd checked out the most likely places, Cam was supposed to have been working the streets.

What if Cam hoped to find Tony through Mattie?

"Can I help you?" Mattie asked the tall man standing on her porch and blocking the path to her car.

"My name is Cam. I work with Dominic Jeffries."

He pulled out a wallet and showed her his ID. Visions of uniformed men bringing bad news to family and friends made her knees wobble. "Is Dom hurt?"

Shaking his head, Cam took her hand in both of his. "Mattie, I'm here because Dominic is frantic. He's told me everything. We've doubled up, trying to find your brother. He's on his way to Tony's apartment right now."

Assured that Dom was okay, she scrambled to think straight. To remember where she was headed and why she hadn't called Dom to meet her there. "I've already told Dom that I'm not—"

"Guapo knows Tony snitched him out," Cam interrupted. "He's put out a bounty. $100,000. Do you understand what men will do for that kind of money? If Tony's seen by any of his old buddies, he's not going to last long." Cam gripped her arms, squeezing her so tightly she gasped. "I need you to tell me where he is. Now."

"I—I—" Wrenching out of Cam's grip, Mattie raised a hand to her forehead. "Tony's at the hospital," she cried. "He went to visit—"

"The D.A. who was attacked."

"He wanted to see her—"

Cam shook his head. "We need to get Tony into protective custody as soon as possible."

Protective custody. Oh God. "Okay, okay. Let's go."

Mattie followed Cam down the walkway to a four-door sedan, clearly police issued. As soon as she was seated, she took her cell phone out of her purse.

Cam pulled onto the road. "What are you doing?"

"I want to call Dom. There may be men waiting for Tony at the apartment and he should get out of there."

"Here, let me do it."

Mattie stared at the hand he held out. "Why?"

Cam's gaze was unflinching. "Because Dom told me about the fight you had, Mattie," he said softly. "It's why he didn't come here himself. He—I'm sorry, but he doesn't want to talk to you."

Hurt ratcheted up her guilt. Of course he didn't want to see her. She'd been nothing but trouble for him. "He thinks this is my fault, doesn't he? Because I didn't help him bring in Tony sooner."

Cam said nothing. Slowly, Mattie handed him the phone and turned to stare out the window. Had she endangered Tony when she'd just been trying to protect him?

"I have to call my daughter when you're done. If I'm going to be with Tony, I need to arrange for someone to pick her up."

Cam held up a finger. "Hey, Dom," he said into the phone. "We've got him. He's at the hospital, and Mattie and I are on our way right now. We'll meet you at the station. Oh, and Mattie's worried about picking up her daughter. Can you do that and bring her to the station with you?" He nodded at Mattie and held the phone away from his ear. "He wants to know where she is?"

Confusion came first. Then unease. Then fear.

Dom knew where Jordan was. She was with her grand-parents, exactly where Dom had arranged for her to be.

When she failed to answer, Cam jiggled the phone im-patiently but shifted his gaze to the road in order to pass a slow-moving car. "I assume she's at a friend's house?"

Staring at his profile, Mattie slowly said, "Yes—she's at a friend's. The Malcolm family. 482 West Harbor Boule-vard," Mattie fabricated. Digging her fingers into the edge of her seat, she forced herself not to lean away from him as she wanted to.

Continuing with his act, Cam nodded. "The Malcolm family," Cam said into the phone, then repeated the address. "You got that? Good."

Mattie didn't take her eyes off him. She was acutely aware of the fear that had grown inside her, but she was also aware of a strong sense of calm. Keeping her expression closed, she finally understood what made Dom so reluctant to wear his emotions on his sleeve. Sometimes the more you cared, the more you had to pretend you didn't.

Cam snapped the phone closed and tucked it into his shirt pocket. "He's got it covered. He'll meet us there." He reached out and placed his hand on her knee, patting it. "Don't look so worried, Mattie. Tony should be fine at the hospital until we get to him."

She stared at his hand, wanting to throw it off her. Instead, she said, "May I have my phone? I should call Tony and tell him where to meet me."

Annoyance flashed across Cam's face, but he retrieved the cell phone and handed it to her. "Tell him to meet us at the administration desk."

Fumbling slightly, Mattie opened the phone and dialed Tony's cell phone.

"Mattie."

Mattie closed her eyes in relief when she heard Tony's voice. "Tony. I need you to meet me at the administration desk. I'm going to meet you with a friend of mine."

"Your friend the cop? Dominic? No way, Mattie. You know he—"

"No, not Dominic. A man named Cam. I trust him, Tony. He says your life is in danger. That Sabon knows. After you see Linda, come to the administration desk."

There was momentary pause on the line. "But Mattie, you know I can't see—"

"That's right, after. Okay. I'll see you then." Mattie hung up the phone and tucked it into her purse. Turning her head back toward the passenger window, she stared at the blurring scenery and prayed that Tony would understand her warning and leave for someplace safe. "He's going to meet us there."

She sensed Cam's touch before she felt it on her hair. "Oh, Mattie. I wish you hadn't done that. I know Dom's got Linda on guard. No way would Tony be able to see her on his own."

She closed her eyes briefly before turning toward him. With almost casual ease, he pointed a gun at her while he deftly navigated the car with his other hand. The gun even looked malevolent and she felt her fear spike. She shrugged. "I've never been very good under pressure."

"Well, I can safely assume your brother is going to call Dom, who's then going to come after us. He's going to have to find us first, of course, and that may or may not take some time. In any event, we're passing Go and going directly to Jail. You're going to tell Sabon that your brother was the informant. He can take care of your brother from there."

Refusing to rub the sharp ache at her temple, she tilted her chin up. "And what makes you think I'll say anything to help you?"

Cam slid the gun barrel down her cheek and throat, then

wound a lazy circle around her breast. "I have ways of making people talk, Mattie. Frank Manelli knows that better than anyone."

Dom was speeding toward Mattie's house, sirens blaring, when his cell phone rang.

It was the station dispatcher. "Detective Jeffries, we have a caller trying to reach you who says it's an emergency. His name is Tony—"

"Put him on," Dom urged, not slowing down.

"Transferring."

"Hello? Hello?" The panic in the man's voice was unmistakable.

Terror unlike he'd ever known tightened Dom's chest until he could barely breathe. He forced himself to picture Mattie, then Jordan. Since losing them was not an option, neither was giving in to his fear. When he spoke, his voice was controlled. "Tony, this is Dominic Jeffries."

"He has Mattie," Tony shouted. "She just called me. Talked to me about seeing Linda. I—I—she knows I couldn't go in to see her because of the guard but—"

"Whoa, whoa. Just calm down, Tony. Who has Mattie? Where did she call you from?"

"She was on her cell phone. I think she was in a car. She said she was on her way to the hospital—Sutter Memorial Hospital—with a guy named Cam. Do you know who that is?"

His fingers tightened on the steering wheel. Damn Cam to hell and back. He would pay for touching Mattie. For even daring to frighten her. "Yes, I know who it is. Are you still at the hospital, Tony?"

"Yes! I waited, just in case they showed up. But she hasn't. She was warning me that they were coming, but she didn't show up!"

With a quick look in his rearview mirror, Dom braked hard, wheels skidding as he maneuvered his vehicle into a sharp U-turn and sped toward the hospital. "You were the CI who gave us the information on Guapo."

"Yes. But—"

"Cam is a fellow officer." Dom passed several cars and switched lanes. He pressed down harder on the accelerator. "He's likely responsible for the death of another police officer, as well as Judge Butler, Grant Falcon, Guapo's defense attorney, and the assault on Linda. Given the parties involved, he has to be working for Guapo. If Cam was bringing Mattie to you, it was so he could take you somewhere. Do you know where that would be?"

"To Sabon. He'd bring us to Sabon."

"Since the raid, Guapo's compound has been shut down. I have no idea where—"

"There's a warehouse Sabon uses now for large deliveries. Cam would meet him there. Where are you?"

"I'm almost at the hospital, but tell me where the warehouse is. I'll send a car for you."

"I'm going with you."

"No," Dom snapped. "Just tell me where it is."

"This is all my fault. Mattie being in danger. Linda. Judge Butler. Pick me up. You may be able to use me as a negotiating tool. Trade me for Mattie."

"I'm not going to do that. Mattie wouldn't want that. And I sure can't have backup officers with me and bring you to the scene. They'll never let you in."

"Then we'll go alone. I'm not telling you where the warehouse is. Pick me up."

"Tony—" Dom cursed when he got a dial tone. Dom threw his cell phone on the passenger seat and took a hard right. The hospital was two blocks away.

Chapter 17

With Tony directing him, Dominic made it to the warehouse in less than ten minutes. He drove his truck in slowly, sirens quiet. He didn't want to spook Cam, but he almost panicked when he saw Sabon's red Camaro parked next to Cam's car.

"Backup is on its way," he told Tony. "Wait here and tell them that there are two suspects inside, armed and dangerous."

"No! I know Sabon. I can help—"

Barely hearing him, Dominic exited the car and moved toward a rusting, blue metal door at the south end of the building. Drawing his weapon, he paused outside the door, his back to the wall and took in several deep breaths.

He whirled at the sound of footsteps behind him, cursing when he saw Tony. The younger man froze momentarily, then took position next to the other side of the door. He was sweating, his face reflecting his fear, but there was courage there, too, as well as resolve.

"Get back in the car," Dom snapped, already knowing the man wouldn't listen to him.

"No."

You were right to give him your loyalty, Mattie. Assessing his options, he cursed one more time, but with little heat. "Here."

When Tony looked at him, Dom handed him his gun. "You know how to use it?"

Tony undid the safety and nodded. "Point and shoot. Even I can do that. But what about you?"

Dom reached for the smaller gun he carried in his leg holster, hoping that giving Tony the larger and more reliable of the two would keep him safe. Besides, Dom's backup had saved his life on more than one occasion; he was banking on it doing so again. "Why bother having one when two are so much better? Now listen to me. Cam is an expert shot. There's no way we can both get in there without him taking one of us out. We need to keep them guessing. Go around back and see if you can find a way in."

"The red Camaro—"

Dom nodded. "I know. It's Sabon's. It's two against two, so you go around back, do you understand?"

Tony swiped at his forehead, unintentionally pointing the wavering gun at Dom. "Okay, okay." He moved past Dom, but Dom grabbed his arm.

"Get Mattie out of here. No matter what you hear. Whether you know where I am or not. Got it?"

"She won't leave knowing you're here."

"Then don't tell her I'm here."

Tony swallowed then nodded. "Just get your ass out alive. Because Mattie'll hate me if anything happens to you."

Unbelievably, Dom felt the smile spread across his face. "Mattie couldn't hate you. Get her out, and if I can't do it myself, give my daughter a kiss for me."

They stared at one another, respect and understanding passing between them. With a final nod, Tony took off toward the back of the building.

Dom took a deep breath, got into position, then swung the door open. "Police," he shouted. "Get your hands up."

There was no answer. No sound or sign of movement. Carefully, he entered the warehouse only to find a vast room filled with boxes. He ducked behind a crate to establish cover. The ache in his side flashed intense and quick, a sharp stab underneath his ribs that made him cringe.

Not now.

Someone began to whistle "God Save The Queen."

The bastard was playing with him. "Where's Mattie, Cam?"

Cam stepped into view, keeping one arm extended, his gun pointed toward the back of the crate he'd been hiding behind. "What do you think, Dom? You think you can shoot me before I put a bullet through her brain?"

"Why, Cam?" Dom breathed, unable to disguise his confusion. "You're one of us."

"Poor Dom. You really are out of the loop on this one, aren't you? Badass undercover cop didn't even know that the men he's worked with for years aren't any better than the scum he's trying to lock up."

Not abandoning his cover, Dom snorted. "Men? Who are you talking about, Cam? Frank? Joel? Because I don't buy that about Joel. I never will."

Cam shrugged. "He said your name as he died, you know. Right before he said Tawny's."

A red haze momentarily blinded him. "I'm going to kill you, Cam," Dom said. "And what you did to Frank is going to look like child's play in comparison."

Cam smiled. "Ah, so you found old Frank? He wasn't so pretty, was he? He sure was a tough dude, though. It took him a few hours before he started begging. I'm betting Mattie'll beg a lot sooner."

"Where is she?"

"Why don't you come and find out?" Quick as a rattlesnake, Cam ducked behind the crate. At that very moment, Tony darted from behind his own crate and moved closer to Cam. Dom hissed in a breath, knowing that Cam would hear him coming from a mile away. Sure enough, Dom heard the sound of Cam's gun being cocked and saw the extension of his arms taking aim just as Tony moved into range.

"Tony, run," Dom shouted. Eyes wide, Tony dove out of sight. Leaping out from behind the crate, Dom rushed Cam just as his insides exploded. Pain knifed through him, causing him to curl over and land on the cement floor with so much force that he grunted. His gun skidded out of his hand and he tried to crawl for it, but the nausea was so bad he almost threw up. Insides still heaving, he saw Cam's legs out of his periphery.

"No," Dom gasped out, trying to hold on to consciousness. "Where's... Mattie..."

Cam kicked Dom's gun out of his reach and crouched down next to him. Grabbing Dom's hair, he pulled his head back until his neck muscles screamed in protest. He grinned. "Your ulcer acting up again, L.B.?" Quick as lightning, Cam punched Dom in the side. Dom screamed out in pain and fury, trying to grab hold of Cam with numb fingers. "Looks like I fooled you again. Mattie's entertaining Sabon, Dom. But I don't think she's having a very good time."

Before Dom could even try to respond, Cam pushed his head toward the floor. Blinding pain exploded behind Dom's eyelids and everything went blank.

Mattie came awake by degrees. The first thing she became aware of was pain. In her head. In her body. Even her fingernails ached. She struggled to open her eyes, blinking until the blurred outline of a man came into focus. Fear filled her as she realized she was lying prone on a hard, cold surface, and that Michael Sabon was straddling her, staring at her with menacing intensity and a mocking grin.

"Where's Tony—" she managed to choke out.

"That's what I was hoping you could tell me."

"I don't know."

Sabon's face twisted into cruel lines. He grabbed her hair in one hand and yanked back her head. Mattie moaned in terror when she felt the hard edge of a gun barrel shoved under her chin.

A shout rang out behind her. Sabon released her hair. "Shut up!" he hissed.

Voices drifted in from the other room. She distinctly heard a man shout "police."

"Help—" she screamed immediately, just before Sabon shoved his free hand over her mouth. With both hands occupied, he could barely subdue Mattie as she arched and wriggled to escape him. He struck her in the temple with the gun, splitting open her head so that blood immediately trickled into her eyes. He laid down his gun and grabbed both of her wrists in one of his and stretched them over her head. As she continued to struggle, Sabon shifted the hand covering her mouth to her throat, squeezing so tight that she instantly lost air.

Her wheezing gasps drowned out the voices in the other room and her vision tunneled into a small pinpoint of light. Her muscles went limp and she could feel herself losing consciousness just as Sabon released her.

"Try anything else and I will kill you. Then I'll kill your daughter. Your mother. Anyone you've ever been friends with. Do you hear me?"

Limp and shaking, gasping for air, Mattie's head lolled

back and forth on the floor. Although she strained to hear them, the voices had quieted. Was anyone still there? Her stomach rolled when Sabon released her wrists, and ran his hands over her breasts and between her legs before leaning closer. "Don't think anyone's coming to rescue you," he whispered. "If anything, Cam probably has your brother in tow. I can't wait to get my hands on him."

Leaning away but still holding her wrists, he slapped her. Instead of subduing her, the sharp pain, like a vial of smelling salts, seemed to bring her awareness back. Her blurry vision focused until she could see every pore on his face. Turning her head slightly, Mattie honed in on the gun that Sabon had left on the floor.

He grabbed her chin, digging his fingers into her flesh so hard that she whimpered. "That's right. You're going to make noise. You're going to scream when your brother gets here. I'll make sure I hurt you really good so he'll know for certain—no one messes with Guapo or his brother. In fact, I don't want to wait. I want you to scream now."

Pressing her lips together mutinously, Mattie shook her head.

"Scream!" he shouted.

Come on, she thought. *Lose control. Be sloppy.*

As if he heard her thoughts, Sabon sat back even farther, balancing on his knees and leaving his groin vulnerable. He raised his hand to slap her again and Mattie's mind screamed "now." Curling her knee into her chest as hard as she could, she relished Sabon's howl of pain, but she didn't pause. Pressing the flat of her foot against his stomach, she pushed out with all her might and sent him flying. With a slithering lunge, she got hold of the gun, only to scream when Sabon's foot pressed onto her arm. He stomped on her arm again but Mattie refused to uncurl her fingers from the butt of the gun. Instead, when Sabon grabbed her by the hair to lift her up, she twisted her arm out from under his foot and slammed the gun into his kneecap. With a yell, he released her and stumbled. Scrambling to her feet, Mattie pointed the gun at him. Quick as lightning, Sabon reached in his jacket and flipped out a razor blade, one that was relatively small but sharp enough to do what he had in mind. Gut her. Kill her. Then kill Tony.

Hands shaking, Mattie flinched when Sabon sliced the knife toward her.

He just laughed and moved closer.

She commanded her feet to move back. Her finger to pull the trigger. But her gaze was mesmerized by the slashing arcs of the blade, her body paralyzed by shock and fear.

The door to the room was flung open. Sabon turned at the same time Mattie saw Tony stumble into the room. "Mattie," he yelled.

With an animalistic roar, Sabon launched himself at Tony. Tony lifted his arms straight out, but he dropped the gun he was holding as soon as Sabon made contact. Even as Sabon stabbed Tony with the knife, Mattie couldn't force the scream from her open mouth. As Tony dropped to the floor, Sabon kicked him several times in the ribs and in the face.

Her brother wasn't moving. He didn't make a sound.

Sabon looked at her, raised the bloody blade, and waggled it at her. "What's a matter, lady? Can't pull the trigger? Too bad your daughter is going to be left an orphan," he taunted. "Tony always loved the little brat. Now, to finish this little bastard off before we get back to what we started."

Sabon pulled his arm back to plunge the blade into Tony's chest.

Suddenly Mattie's body came to life. Jordan wasn't going to be an orphan. Even if she and Tony didn't make it out of here alive, she'd have a father. One who'd insure her happiness. She didn't doubt Dominic's ability to love and care for his daughter. Not anymore.

"I'm sorry, Dominic," she said out loud. "I'm sorry I didn't trust you when I should have."

Sabon turned at the sound of her voice, a puzzled expression on his face. When she took two steps forward, he frowned.

She didn't warn him to stop.

She didn't give him a chance to back off.

She just pulled the trigger without an ounce of hesitation and watched Sabon fall to the ground.

Chapter 18

Pain throbbed steadily at Dom's temple, tempting him to slide into the darkness once again, but he refused to go. He tried to move his arms and legs, but they remained still, encased in quicksand that was about to swallow him whole.

Desperately, he opened his eyes, blinking until his vision finally cleared.

Dom stared at the man standing before him, leaning against a stack of crates with his arms crossed over his chest. "You killed Joel, didn't you? You planted the drugs?"

Straightening, Cam walked toward him. "Sorry, bloke. I can't take credit for the drugs." Cam pulled at the rope binding Dom's wrists together, testing to make sure they had no give. "I'm afraid those were already there when Joel and I had our little disagreement."

"Disagreement about what? How soon you'd be going to hell?"

"Tsk tsk, now. Let's not make this personal, Dom. It's not."

Disbelief couldn't have hit him any stronger. "You trying to kill me, Mattie and her brother? I take that personally."

"Well you shouldn't. This is all Frank Manelli's fault, you know." Pulling the gun from his holster, Cam crouched and shoved it underneath Dom's chin. "He cheated on Grace again and again. After he was out of the picture, I poured my heart out to her and you know what she said? That she could never love me the way she loves him. That she filed for divorce to scare him straight." Cam looked at Dom, his confusion obvious, but he didn't lower the gun. "How stupid is that?"

"So you tortured him? Stripped the skin from his body?"

"Maybe I enjoyed that a little too much, but in truth I was counting on Guapo's men getting rid of him. Only my plan backfired. I needed to know the confidential informant's identity, Dom, or Guapo was going to come after me."

"You know the CI's identity now. Go. Tell Guapo. Let him come after Tony himself."

He shook his head then stroked the barrel of his gun down Dom's cheek. "Don't play with me, Dom. You know I have to take him to Guapo. But first I have to kill you and Mattie."

Cam straightened, lifted the gun, and pointed it at Dom.

"At least tell me—why Joel?"

Cam laughed. "The lieutenant would be proud of you, L.B. No flinching or begging from you. But that's why you can't understand, Dom. You're like Robocop. You didn't even understand about Joel and Tawny. But Grace—" He took a deep, pained breath. "I love her, man. Everything I've done, I've done for her."

Robocop? Dom felt all right. Despite what Cam or anyone else thought. "Joel understood, even if I couldn't. So why'd you kill him?"

"He didn't understand," Cam roared, his eyes turning wild. "Otherwise he would never have tried to help Frank. My only chance with Grace was getting Frank out of the picture, and I had the perfect opportunity. He's not just a cheat, Dom, he's a thief. He took the drugs from Guapo during the raid and Joel found out about it. He made Manelli give him the drugs, then was going to turn him in."

"How'd you get involved, Cam?"

"He called me. Told me the whole thing. Asked me to take a freaking report and book the drugs into evidence!"

"Why not do it? Manelli's reputation would have been destroyed. He would've gone to prison—"

"And she would have waited for him. No. I wanted Frank dead. And he would have been if Joel had just let Guapo have him."

"So you killed Joel?"

Cam frowned, bewilderment flashing across his face. "No. No, I never meant to hurt him. That—it was an accident. But once Joel was gone, I tried to set the record straight with Guapo. I told him about Manelli. Instead of taking care of Frank, he decided to use me to find out who the CI was. Only Manelli couldn't identify him and I had no clue who it was. How's that for a laugh?"

"So Falcon. Linda Delaney. Even Judge Butler?"

"Falcon wasn't my doing. All the D.A. and the judge had to do was tell me who it was, but they wouldn't. And for who? A two-time druggie?"

"A two-time druggie who was trying to turn his life around."

"You don't know—" Cam's hand jerked at the sound of a gunshot. They stared at one another.

"No," Dom whispered. With a roar of fury, he struggled against his binds.

Don't die, Mattie-mine. Don't leave me. Our daughter needs us and I need you, too. More than I ever thought possible.

"Damn," Cam said. He rushed to a side door, opened it, and peered outside. "Sabon!" he shouted. "Sabon, answer me."

No answer came.

That was good. It slowed the frantic beating of Dom's pulse. It enabled Dom to start thinking again. "Cam," he called, praying Tony had found Mattie and they'd escaped. "Did you ever think that Grace might've been scared? That she really did love you?"

Still holding the door open, Cam glanced at him. "What the hell are you talking about now?"

"Frank hurt her, Cam. Maybe she was just reluctant to get involved with another cop. But Frank's out of the picture now, just like you wanted. You still have a chance with her, Cam. You can leave. Just disappear."

"And how am I supposed to have Grace if I disappear?" he spat back.

Dom took a deep breath. "I don't know. But after this, there's no going back. We were friends, Cam. Do the right thing. Please."

Cam stared at Dom and slowly smiled. "Sorry, Dom. There's already no going back. I guess this is it. Our final game. Who still has a pulse out there? Is it Mattie and her brother, or the dirty drug dealer?"

"Damn it, Cam. Wait—" Dom let out a long roar as Cam disappeared. He heard the turning of a lock.

Immediately, Dom began working at his binds again but Cam had restrained him well. He looked around for something—anything—he could use to work the ropes free. Eyes zooming in on the crate Cam had leaned against, he used his body weight to turn the chair. Inch by meager inch, he managed to work himself toward it until it was directly behind him and he could drag his bound wrists across the edge.

It took precious moments for her to rouse Tony and get him out of the warehouse. Supporting his weight, they stumbled outside. When she saw Dom's truck parked haphazardly with the doors open, she forced herself to walk past it.

Everything Cam had said was a lie. She should never have believed that Dom would turn his back on her for any reason, let alone a fight.

But where was he? And did he know about Cam?

She lowered Tony to the ground as gently as she could, acutely aware of his moans of pain. "I'll be right back, Tony. I have to get Dom."

As she rose to her feet, Tony grabbed her wrist. "Wait, Mattie— Think of Jordan. She needs you."

"I have to help him!" Mattie shouted as she managed to break free. She ran toward a blue metal door kitty-corner from the one they'd exited. "Please, please," she whispered. "Don't let Dom be hurt."

She reached for the door handle and flung the door open. The scream ripped out of her throat like the bullet she'd used to kill Sabon.

Before she could veer away, Cameron Blake, his face contorted into a cold mask of rage, grabbed her, whirled her around and got her in a chokehold. "I'll snap her neck," he warned Tony, who'd somehow gotten to his feet and been right behind her. Her brother's gaze met hers, then darted over her shoulder even as he swayed, blinking and trying to hang on to consciousness.

"Don't hurt her," Tony gasped out.

"Worry about yourself, my friend. I'm assuming you got the better of Sabon, but unfortunately for all of us, I still need you. You're going to talk to Guapo's men and you're going to confess what you did or I'm going to hurt your sister here."

Several loud thuds echoed from inside, making them all jerk. Mattie could barely hear a voice shouting her name.

It was Dominic.

He was alive and still trying to save her.

Tony shook his head. "They'll kill her. You know they will."

"No—" Mattie screamed, struggling for a few seconds before the band around her throat tightened. With a jerk of his arm, Cam lifted her off her feet and cut off her air supply. She gasped and wheezed, clawing at his arm even as her vision blurred. She could just make out Tony stumbling forward before he lost his balance and fell to his knees.

Please, no. Not now. Not like this.

Immediately, the vise around her throat loosened and she sucked in breath.

"Better her than me. Now let's go. Into the car."

With an arm still around Mattie, Cam frog-marched her to Tony. With his free hand, he gripped her brother by his shirt collar and dragged him up. Another thud from inside had him turning his head to glance behind him. "Now," he gritted.

He shoved Tony toward his car, then threw him the keys. They fell at Tony's feet. "Open the trunk."

The thuds from inside stopped.

"Now," Cam screamed, jerking Mattie off her feet once more.

"Okay, okay," Tony said. He picked up the keys, fumbled at the lock for several seconds, then finally opened the trunk.

"Get in," Cam ordered.

Clumsily, he did.

Cam began to drag her toward the open trunk as well. "We're going for a ride."

"No." Mattie wriggled, throwing herself from side to side. If she got into that trunk, she'd never see Dom again. She'd never see Jordan. And that was not acceptable.

Her shoes scraped against the pavement as he continued to drag her. When she flung herself forward, however, his grip slipped and he struggled for balance. Instinctively, she tucked her chin into her neck and bit into the flesh of his forearm.

He shouted and pulled away, but Mattie hung on, grinding her teeth in even deeper until a sudden blow to her head made her jaw loosen. He swung her around, and slapped her so hard she staggered into the car and thumped her head against it. Pain exploded in the back of her head and she felt her feet give way beneath her. Slowly, she slid to the ground.

All she saw were four jean-clad legs walking toward her, the force of the blow causing her to see double. But wait—

Those weren't four of Cam's legs. Those were two pairs of legs. That meant…

Forcing her chin up, she saw two large forms wrestling. Dom and Cam, so comparably matched in size and strength. But even in her dazed state, Mattie could see the rage on Dom's face as well as the small spark of fear that had formed on Cam's.

She couldn't see individual movements. Couldn't separate one punch from another. But she could see the way Cam's head jerked back over and over again until he was backing away from Dom and into the car behind her, like a heavyweight fighter on the ropes.

"I'll kill you for hurting her," Dom shouted. "You're dead, do you hear me? You're dead."

"Dominic," she tried to shout, but it came out as a whisper. She flinched when she felt something grab her.

"It's me. It's Tony." Her brother slumped against her. Even as Mattie pulled him close, she called out for Dominic, her voice getting stronger with each word until she was screaming.

He finally heard her. With a shove, he pushed Cam to the ground and knelt beside Mattie. Gently, he pulled her from Tony's arms and embraced her. "Are you okay, baby?"

She nodded. Over his shoulder, she saw Cam stagger to

his feet and start to run toward the main road. "Dominic," she croaked, "he's getting away."

"He's hurt and he doesn't have a gun." He gestured to a gun he had tucked into his pants, then gently turned her face towards his. "You're what matters to me, Mattie, and I'm not leaving your side."

"But—"

He shook his head. "Shhh. It's okay, baby. Where's he going to go? He'll get his due. I have no doubt about that."

He leaned back against the car with her and though he tried to hide it, she saw him wince. "Are you hurt?" It was a stupid question, given the fact that his face was bruised, swollen, and cut up. It was what she couldn't see that worried her, however, and she immediately got to her knees and began running her hands over him.

"My shoulder," he gritted from between clenched teeth. "I think I dislocated it trying to get the hell out of that room."

"Oh, no."

He shook his head and put his good arm around her, pulling her back toward him. "I've been hurt worse. It's nothing compared to how I felt when I couldn't get to you." He leaned forward and looked at Tony, whose head was tipped back, his eyes closed. "Tony was really brave. He wasn't going to let anything happen to you. I couldn't have asked for a better partner."

Tony smiled slightly. "You're just saying that because I'm going to be your—" he hissed with pain as he shifted his legs "—your star witness as soon as the district attorney charges Cam with a whole helluva lot of crimes."

"Not my star witness," Dom said. "I'm not talking you into anything, Tony."

When he looked at Mattie, checking for her reaction, she smiled. "It is Tony's decision, but I trust your advice, whatever that is." Careful of his shoulder, she laid her head on his chest, her hand covering his strong heartbeat. A few minutes later, when they heard the sirens in the distance, Mattie turned her face into his neck. "I—I killed him. I shot Sabon." Her voice wavered as shock settled in.

"Good," was Dom's only response. Closing her eyes, she clung to him even tighter.

To the man who cared about her safety above all else.

Chapter 19

Mattie was a killer but she couldn't feel remorse for her actions. Michael Sabon had tried to hurt her and her family, and she wouldn't hesitate to kill again in order to stop him. Unfortunately, however, when you killed the brother of a renowned drug king, especially when your brother was already wanted by the same drug king, it tended to complicate things.

Even though Linda had regained consciousness several days ago, she was still pumped full of drugs. Sleeping now in her hospital room, she wouldn't remember Tony's tender kiss. He slipped an envelope that contained both Mattie's letter and his own, under her pillow.

Dom had been right. Cam hadn't had anywhere to go. Police had found him and booked him into jail. Even though he'd been given protective custody as a former police officer, he'd been killed in his cell, his throat slit. Although his cell mate had claimed self-defense, no one doubted that he'd been acting under Guapo's orders.

As for them, Mattie, Tony and Jordan were officially being entered into the witness protection program. They couldn't be certain that, before he'd been killed, Cam hadn't told even one person that Tony was the confidential informant who'd sold Guapo out. It was either witness protection or spending the rest of their lives fearing that Guapo's men would someday come for them. They'd be leaving Sacramento tomorrow morning.

"We should be going," Mattie whispered to Tony.

Together they walked to the door. "I've always wanted to see more of the United States."

She nodded and linked arms with him, trying to be brave just as he was. "It'll be exciting, not knowing where we're going. An adventure."

Out in the hallway, Dom and Jordan barely looked up from their game of thumb wars. Jordan giggled when Dom "lost" and feigned outrage.

"You've got a ringer here, Mattie."

"Don't I know it." She ruffled Jordan's hair, so proud of her daughter and the man she loved. When he'd told Mattie and Tony about the witness protection program, he'd thrown in one other detail—that he wanted to come with them. "Can you be a cop in the witness protection program?" He'd looked at her with steady eyes and said, "I don't see why not. But even if I can't, I still want to come with you anyway."

It shouldn't have been enough. Law enforcement was in his blood, and even if he quit altogether, he'd likely made enemies that might come after him. No one doubted that if Guapo ever found out where Mattie or Tony were, anyone with them would be in danger, too. But instead of bringing that all up, Mattie had done what Dom was finally doing— she'd trusted their love to get them through anything.

They were waiting to tell Jordan that Dom was her father simply because it might be one change too many for her to handle. But in the past week, Jordan had already formed a strong bond with the man she called "Dommy." It would only get stronger with time.

Dom stood, gave her a hug, then nodded at Tony. "Everything go okay in there?"

"She never woke up. I only wish I could tell her..." Tony shrugged. "Even with the letter I left, she'll never really know how much she meant to me."

Mattie took his hand. "She'll know, Tony."

After squeezing her hand, Tony tickled Jordan, eliciting squeals of laughter, then began walking down the hall backwards. "Come on, squirt."

Watching them, Mattie couldn't help but sigh.

Dom tipped her chin up. "Hey there. No worrying now. It'll be good for him. A whole new start. Plus, with all the kids we're going to have, he's not going to have much time to get into trouble."

She was drowning in the brilliant blue of his eyes. The color still reminded her of the sea—turbulent at times, peaceful at others, but always rocking. With Dom, her life would never come with guarantees, but she knew a good bet when she saw one. Mattie smiled. "Oh. Lots of kids, huh?"

"Sure. A dozen at least."

"And you know this how?"

"The future's looking pretty clear to me right now. In fact, I'm sensing something else." He gave an exaggerated frown and lifted a hand to his forehead. "Wait, it's something about where we're going to be living soon."

She slapped at his arm. "Did you find out where we're going?"

He lowered his arm only to place both hands on her shoulders. "No, babe. That's not how it works. But it doesn't matter where we go, as long as the state meets some simple requirements."

"Which are?"

"Don't you know?" He leaned down, kissed her gently, and whispered in her ear, "Broad streets, a wraparound porch, blue shutters and—"

"—the best apple pie ever," they finished together.

"I love you, Mattie. I'm so lucky to have found you again."

"And I'm so lucky you found me."

Hand in hand, with Jordan and Tony in front of them, Mattie's family walked toward home.

* * * * *

ROMANTIC
SUSPENSE

COMING NEXT MONTH

Available September 27, 2011

You can find more information on upcoming
Harlequin® titles, free excerpts and more at
www.HarlequinInsideRomance.com.

HRSCNM0911

REQUEST YOUR FREE BOOKS!
2 FREE NOVELS PLUS 2 FREE GIFTS!

 Harlequin

ROMANTIC
SUSPENSE

Sparked by Danger, Fueled by Passion.

YES! Please send me 2 FREE Harlequin® Romantic Suspense novels and my 2 FREE gifts (gifts are worth about $10). After receiving them, if I don't wish to receive any more books, I can return the shipping statement marked "cancel." If I don't cancel, I will receive 4 brand-new novels every month and be billed just $4.49 per book in the U.S. or $5.24 per book in Canada. That's a saving of at least 14% off the cover price! It's quite a bargain! Shipping and handling is just 50¢ per book in the U.S. and 75¢ per book in Canada.* I understand that accepting the 2 free books and gifts places me under no obligation to buy anything. I can always return a shipment and cancel at any time. Even if I never buy another book, the two free books and gifts are mine to keep forever.

240/340 HDN FEFR

Name   (PLEASE PRINT)

Address   Apt. #

City   State/Prov.   Zip/Postal Code

Signature (if under 18, a parent or guardian must sign)

Mail to the **Reader Service:**

IN U.S.A.: P.O. Box 1867, Buffalo, NY 14240-1867
IN CANADA: P.O. Box 609, Fort Erie, Ontario L2A 5X3

Not valid for current subscribers to Harlequin Romantic Suspense books.

Want to try two free books from another line?
Call 1-800-873-8635 or visit www.ReaderService.com.

* Terms and prices subject to change without notice. Prices do not include applicable taxes. Sales tax applicable in N.Y. Canadian residents will be charged applicable taxes. Offer not valid in Quebec. This offer is limited to one order per household. All orders subject to credit approval. Credit or debit balances in a customer's account(s) may be offset by any other outstanding balance owed by or to the customer. Please allow 4 to 6 weeks for delivery. Offer available while quantities last.

Your Privacy—The Reader Service is committed to protecting your privacy. Our Privacy Policy is available online at www.ReaderService.com or upon request from the Reader Service.

We make a portion of our mailing list available to reputable third parties that offer products we believe may interest you. If you prefer that we not exchange your name with third parties, or if you wish to clarify or modify your communication preferences, please visit us at www.ReaderService.com/consumerschoice or write to us at Reader Service Preference Service, P.O. Box 9062, Buffalo, NY 14269. Include your complete name and address.

HRS11B

*Harlequin Romantic Suspense presents the latest book
in the scorching new* KELLEY LEGACY *miniseries
from best-loved veteran series author Carla Cassidy*

*Scandal is the name of the game as the Kelley family fights
to preserve their legacy, their hearts…and their lives.*

Read on for an excerpt from the fourth title
RANCHER UNDER COVER

*Available October 2011
from Harlequin Romantic Suspense*

"**W**ould you like a drink?" Caitlin asked as she walked
to the minibar in the corner of the room. She felt as if she
needed to chug a beer or two for courage.

"No, thanks. I'm not much of a drinking man," he
replied.

She raised an eyebrow and looked at him curiously as she
poured herself a glass of wine. "A ranch hand who doesn't
enjoy a drink? I think maybe that's a first."

He smiled easily. "There was a six-month period in my
life when I drank too much. I pulled myself out of the bottom of a bottle a little over seven years ago and I've never
looked back."

"That's admirable, to know you have a problem and then
fix it."

Those broad shoulders of his moved up and down in
an easy shrug. "I don't know how admirable it was, all I
knew at the time was that I had a choice to make between
living and dying and I decided living was definitely more
appealing."

She wanted to ask him what had happened preceding
that six-month period that had plunged him into the bottom

of the bottle, but she didn't want to know too much about him. Personal information might produce a false sense of intimacy that she didn't need, didn't want in her life.

"Please, sit down," she said, and gestured him to the table. She had never felt so on edge, so awkward in her life.

"After you," he replied.

She was aware of his gaze intensely focused on her as she rounded the table and sat in the chair, and she wanted to tell him to stop looking at her as if she were a delectable dessert he intended to savor later.

Watch Caitlin and Rhett's sensual saga unfold amidst the shocking, ripped-from-the-headlines drama of the Kelley Legacy miniseries in

RANCHER UNDER COVER

*Available October 2011
only from Harlequin Romantic Suspense,
wherever books are sold.*

♦ Harlequin®

SPECIAL EDITION

Life, Love and Family

Look for
NEW YORK TIMES AND *USA TODAY*
BESTSELLING AUTHOR

KATHLEEN EAGLE

in October!

Recently released and wounded war vet
Cal Cougar is determined to start his recovery—
inside and out. There's no better place than the
Double D Ranch to begin the journey.
Cal discovers firsthand how extraordinary the
ranch really is when he meets a struggling single
mom and her very special child.

ONE BRAVE COWBOY,
available September 27 wherever books are sold!

USA TODAY bestselling author

Carol Marinelli

brings you her new romance

HEART OF THE DESERT

One searing kiss is all it takes for Georgie to know
Sheikh Prince Ibrahim is trouble....

But, trapped in the swirling sands, Georgie finally
surrenders to the brooding rebel prince—yet the
law of his land decrees that she can never
really be his....

Available October 2011.

Available only from Harlequin Presents®.